TO CHRIS

Hope you like the story

THE AALSMEER CONNECTION

BY

ROBERT ELLIS

Published by Lulu.

ISBN 978-0-557-01149-0

Foreword by the Author

When I set out to write this book it was intended to reflect some of my life experiences and some of the restricted information that I have known for years. I was unable to write about some of the projects involved because of the 30 year restriction of the UK National Secrets Act. This book has been 5 years in the writing and is dedicated to my father whom I never really got to spend much time with because of his work with the Ministry of Defence. I have lived and worked in all the places depicted in this book and much of the information is based on personal experience.

Robert Ellis

An extract of the 1911 act and the 1920 and 1989 amendments are set out below.

Terms of the 1911 Act

The act applies in England, Wales, Scotland, Northern Ireland, the Isle of Man, the Channel Islands, and in overseas crown territories and colonies. It also applies to British subjects anywhere else in the world.

- Section 1 - spying. The section is very broadly drafted, and if spying is proved by the prosecution then the section specifically puts the burden of proof on the defendant to show that he/she acted with innocent motives. The maximum sentence is 14 years in prison. British spy George Blake was sentenced to a total of 42 years for offences under this section.

- Section 7 - harbouring spies. 2 years.

- Section 8 - prosecutions under this act require the permission of the Attorney General.

- Section 9 - search warrants. Very unusually, this section gives senior police officers (of the rank superintendent) the power to issue a search warrant in an emergency, if there is no time to obtain one from a judge.

Terms of the 1920 Act

Section 1 - wearing false official uniforms, making false statements, forging official documents, impersonating people, keeping documents or codes etc. without authorisation, and other offences. All punishable by 2 years in prison.

Section 2 - a specific rule of evidence in prosecutions under section 1 of the 1911 Act. Communicating with a foreign agent is admissible as evidence that the defendant intended to help an enemy.

Section 3 - misleading or obstructing a police officer or soldier on duty at a prohibited place. ("Prohibited place" is defined at length by section 3 of the 1911 Act.) 2 years.

Section 6 - refusing to cooperate with a police investigation into a suspected offence under section 1 of the 1911 Act. 2 years.

Section 7 - attempting, inciting, or aiding or abetting an offence under the 1911 or 1920 acts. This section also makes it an offence to *prepare* to commit an offence under either act. This is much wider than ordinary British attempt law.

Section 8 - sets the penalties for the offences under both acts.

] Terms of the 1989 Act

The act applies in England, Wales, Scotland, Northern Ireland, the Isle of Man, the Channel Islands, and in overseas crown territories and colonies. Unusually, the terms of the act apply to affected persons (who are generally employees of the British government) wherever they are in the world.

Section 1 - disclosure of security and intelligence information. It applies only to members of the security and intelligence services, and to others who work with security and intelligence information (and who have been informed that they are affected by section 1).

Section 2 - disclosure of defence information. This section applies only to crown servants and government contractors (defined in section 12)

Section 3 - disclosure of information concerning international relations. This section applies only to crown servants and government contractors.

Section 4 - disclosure of law enforcement information which would assist a criminal or the commission of a crime. This section applies only to crown servants and government contractors.

Section 5 - further disclosure or publication of information obtained in contravention of other sections of the act. It allows, for example, the prosecution of newspapers or journalists who publish secret information leaked to them by a crown servant in contravention of section 3. This section applies to everyone, regardless of whether they are a government employee, or whether they have signed the act.

Section 6 - secret information belonging to foreign governments or international organisations. This section is intended to protect secrets shared by foreign governments and those of international organisations such as the North Atlantic Treaty Organization and Interpol.

Section 7 - defines the circumstances under which a disclosure of secret information is officially published. It is not a crime to disclose information that has been officially published according to the mechanism described in this section.

Section 8 - makes it a crime for a crown servant or government contractor to retain information beyond their official need for it, and obligates them to properly protect secret information from accidental disclosure.

Section 9 - limits the circumstances under which a prosecution under the act may take place. Prosecutions under section 4 require the permission of the Director of Public Prosecutions, or his equivalent in Northern Ireland. Prosecutions under other sections require the permission of the Attorney General or his equivalent in Northern Ireland.

Section 10 - sets the penalties for contravening the act. Persons convicted under sections 4,5, and 8 are subject to six months in prison and a fine; persons convicted under other sections are subject to two years imprisonment and a fine.

Section 11 - amends existing police legislation, making contraventions of this act arrestable offences and allowing for the issuance of search warrants.

Section 12 - defines who is a crown servant and government contractor. This includes civil servants, members of the government, members of the armed forces and their reserve equivalents (including the Territorial Army), police officers, and employees and contract employees of government departments and agencies defined by the Home Secretary.

Section 15 - makes it a crime for British citizens and crown servants to disclose information abroad which would be illegal for them to do so in the UK. This is intended to cover espionage (where someone travels to a foreign country and discloses secret information to a foreign power) and cases where someone travels to a foreign country and discloses secret information, perhaps to a newspaper. The terms of this section do not apply to disclosures covered by sections 4,5, and 8.

Sections (12,13,14, and 16) are present in the act for technical reasons.

In order for a crime to be committed, the following conditions must apply:

1. the disclosure must not be by means permitted in section 7

2. the person making the disclosure must know, or should know, that their disclosure is unauthorised

3. the disclosure must cause harm to the UK or its interests, or it could reasonably be believed that harm could occur, and

4. the person making the disclosure must know, or should know, that such harm could occur

The sections pertaining to crown servants, intelligence officers, and government contractors apply only to information obtained by that person in the course of their official duties; these sections do not apply if the information was obtained by other means (although section 5 would apply).

It is not a defence under the act that the disclosure is in the national or public interest

Further note by the author.

During the 1950s the government began to recognize that the public wanted access to government documents and introduced the Public Records Act of 1958.

But people interested in government secrets, would have to wait 50 years before the documents were released to the public.

30-year rule

The act was reviewed in 1967 and the waiting time was reduced to 30 years.

Chapter One – Stormy Night

It all started in November 1961. I was travelling to the Hook of Holland on the overnight ferry. I was only 18, and had managed to get a job as a sales rep with a Dutch wholesaler of plants and export horticultural gear. I had already lived there for one year before, when I was just 15. I left school early, and got this exchange student deal, worked there for a pittance, but had a lot of fun and learned fluent Dutch within six months. Never realised till then that I had a natural ear for languages, which was to stand me in good stead later in life.

Being only 18 and having an urge to travel and find my own way in life I was off again on my travels. I had decided to take the ferry from Harwich because I liked the experience of going on a ship and anyway it was too expensive to fly. I went to the bar on the ship and ordered a vodka and lime with ice, thinking it was being adult to stand there and have a quiet drink. Being alone when you travel is interesting, you have time to look around and listen to others. My father always said I was too nosy, always overhearing things I shouldn't.

Dad was always discreet, never telling anyone what he really thought, because he couldn't. He worked for the Ministry of Defence and was used to discretion at the highest level. He would often come home with his briefcase shackled to his wrist, and go into his little room he called his study, lock the door and work on whatever project he had been allocated. I was to learn that he did actually work on highly secret material and was subject to the national secrets act. It all seemed a little farfetched to me.

I decided to take my drink, and sit at one of the tables by the outside of the ship, to watch as we cast off from Harwich docks. It was going to be a rough crossing, so I had indulged myself in a private cabin for the night. Rough seas never have worried me. I quite enjoy to this day the sound and feel of large waves pounding the hull of a ship at sea. I was quite looking forward to having a meal and slipping into my bunk till the morning.

As I sat there watching the port slip away and the mouth of the harbour being negotiated. Two men came and sat at the table behind me. I really didn't notice them until they started talking. The waiter came over and asked if I wanted another drink and I accepted. The men behind me were talking in Dutch, and must have heard me talking in English to the waiter. They continued talking quite loudly. They must have assumed that like most English people, I had no idea how to get my mouth round the gutteral language they speak, let alone understand it. I turned around briefly to check out how many people were in the bar area and at the same time to see who these men were. The one facing me was a chubby character with a round face, blond hair and ruddy complexion, wearing jeans and a brown sweater. I also noticed he had a black briefcase at his feet. The man with his back to me was a much leaner man with dark black hair, and he was wearing a long black leather coat that looked expensive, he wore black shoes and obviously new as they had that shine and crispness reserved for new footwear.

I started to eavesdrop on their conversation whilst pretending to read and fill out the landing documents for the morning. They were talking in the accent reserved for the Jewish sector of Amsterdam called locally " De Jordaan". They started talking about gemstones, and in particular diamonds. When I previously lived in Holland I had befriended a workmate whose father was a diamond cutter in Amsterdam and used to frequently go to his house and be fascinated by his father's knowledge of the gems and the various cuts and weights and qualities. So when these two men started talking about blue white stones, baguette cuts and brilliant cuts, I could picture in my mind what they were discussing.

I assumed they were dealers of some kind doing their routine run over to London to sell their wares and establish contracts of sale. They started ordering cognacs, one of them insisting to the waiter that he deliver a Hennessey Bras Arme', obviously they were affluent dealers indulging in the best.

The one with his back to me started explaining to his colleague that the quality of stones they had to deliver was to be of the highest grade, as their client would not accept anything but the best. It will be the biggest contract we have ever fulfilled he said. His colleague said he doubted he could be sure of getting that many stones together in such a short space of time. "Well we're dead if we don't " said the man sitting behind me.

They started discussing the various qualities that might be acceptable. One of them said something that startled me. "We will be told which flight we will have to be on, and when we get to Berlin we will be paid. We can't afford any mistakes, our lives depend on it! ".

Berlin at that time, was cut off from the rest of Western Europe. Except for an air corridor that the Russians used to annoy the western allies, by buzzing civilian aircraft that used it, and whenever they saw fit, to close it, and annoy the Americans and British governments. It was a major part of the Cold War and at times a flashpoint.

The notion that these men were going to send diamonds for whatever reason to Berlin, intrigued me, and I listened with even more attention than before. "What currency are we being paid in?" asked the man looking at my back. "US Dollars" replied the other. "It will go to the Swiss bank account in Zurich. Then when we do the fourth delivery we can go to the next step of the plan." "I can't wait to get it moving" replied the other. "Have patience my friend, we are going to change the order of things forever in Europe, and that requires the utmost planning and a high degree of calm".

This last exchange left me totally confused as to what on earth they were up to, but I decided to go and eat, before they wised on to the fact that I had overheard them and more importantly, had understood what they had said.

I scarcely remember eating my meal, and I went back to the bar to have a coffee before going to bed. The two men were still there talking, but this time they were obviously telling jokes and quite drunk. So I had a quick coffee, and did not go near where they were sitting deliberately. I went to my cabin and fell into an uneasy sleep. At about 02.15am I woke to feel the ship pounding at the obviously rough weather in the North Sea, and voices outside my cabin which were quite clearly two people having an argument. I was about to open my door to see what was up, but then recognised the voices as those of the men I had overheard. One said to the other "If you think I'm going to put my life on the line, to please some Russian bureaucrat just for the sake of dollars then you better think again." The other said "you will be dead if you don't anyway" and he laughed. The first man said "It had better work, if we don't get those plans to them, the diamonds will never be paid for". The second man replied "my friend don't worry, we have people on the inside of the British security and Ministry of Defence at the highest levels. We will get those Blue Streak plans don't you fret."

Blue Streak! Blue Streak! Oh my god! I know that name I thought to myself. I stood transfixed at the door of my cabin, racking my brains to recollect where I had heard that name before. Then it hit me my father had brought papers home a few weeks before I left on this trip, and I had quite innocently walked into his room one Saturday afternoon he hadn't heard me enter. I approached his seat and saw on the desk a red folder marked M.O.D. and the government seal on it. " Top Secret " in red, and below it " Technical costs dept " " BLUE STREAK PROJECT " He heard me suddenly and yelled "get out of here!" I said I was sorry and fled.

Later, curiosity got the better of me and over dinner I asked "What is Blue Streak dad? " He scowled at me and then realized I had seen the folder and said "it's a project that involves shipping some machinery parts to

Australia, they are going to do some testing at a place called Woomera". I had no idea at that moment where Australia was, except that it was a continental island at the bottom of the globe on all the maps I had seen. Woomera was a place I had no notion of. But he did ask me to keep the name to myself, as it was not for public knowledge, and when dad said these sorts of things in his official voice there was no way I was going to cross the line on that.

So what were these guys doing talking about Blue Streak on the ferry to Holland? And where did diamonds fit in? Were they up to no good? Am I imagining this whole thing? I climbed back in to bed my head spinning with all these questions. I tried to sleep and dozed off for few minutes at a time, until the ships PA system crackled to life at 6.00am to announce that breakfast was being served, we were 45 minutes late because of the rough weather. I shaved and washed, put clothes on and lurched my way to the restaurant. There were not many people there most were in their cabins throwing up due to the weather. I did not spot the men, so sat down and enjoyed a hearty breakfast, with lots of hot coffee.

I went back to my cabin, packed my suitcase, and looked out of the porthole, to see if I could see the coastline of Holland, but it was so murky, I couldn't make out much. I sat there with the questions still going round and round in my head. Should I ring my father when I got to my host family's house in Aalsmeer? Or should I just forget the whole thing and assume I had not heard what they had discussed? I decided the latter course of action was the way to go, after all, who would believe me? I didn't even know who they were! The authorities would never believe the rantings of some silly 18 yr old kid. They would tell me condescendingly that I had been reading too many of Ian Fleming's books! And they might be right.

I stood in the immigration queue at Hoek Van Holland, and immediately my mind switched to thinking in Dutch. I greeted the immigration officer in his own tongue, and explained I was going to live and work in Holland again for while. He told me to enjoy my stay as he stamped my passport. Then I looked over my shoulder and one of the men I had overheard was standing right behind me! Had he overheard my fluent Dutch? Did he even recognise me as the person on the table next to them the night before? He gave no indication of recognising me, not even looking my way, so I assumed my vivid imagination had once again got the better of me, and walked off to catch the train to Amsterdam. I was relieved to see both men get in a car outside the port building and drive off.

The rest of the trip was uneventful, except that, looking out of the window of the train at the flat and windswept, stark Dutch countryside, I felt at home, back in my beloved Holland. I was greeted with open arms by my host family that I had stayed with two years before nothing had changed much. The brick built house the same design as the rest of the houses in Hadleystraat, small but cozy, and like most Dutch houses the curtains of the living room are never drawn, so passersby can admire the plants and flowers adorning the window's sills. Their daughter a few years younger than me had blossomed into a pretty young girl and I can't say I wasn't impressed by the cozy hug she gave me when I arrived, only to be introduced to her boyfriend a few moments later. Still, I would catch up with her another time I resolved. I had to go and report to my new boss that afternoon and arrange as to when I was to officially start work.

Aalsmeer is a small town, just 16km south of Amsterdam and close to Schiphol airport, deriving it's main income from flowers, seed production and a unique year round trade forcing Lilacs into flower under glass. The flowers are auctioned daily at the clock auction near the centre of town, then most find their way to the airport and are in the florist shops of London, Paris, Rome, Berlin, and Vienna by the afternoon. Premium prices are paid for these high quality products and the growers make a good living from it. There is a thin peninsula of land called "De Uiterweg" or "De Buurt" as the locals call it. Down the spine of this peninsula, runs a road and a lot of the nurseries and seed producers properties run off this road. At the end of the outcrop of land the road comes to a halt and there is small chain driven ferry that can take you over to the other side of the "Ringvaart" as the canal is called, to join the road to Rijsenhout. Right opposite the ferry there is a hotel and restaurant called "De Uil". It is here a lot of the growers gather after work to have a Jenever or coffee to discuss business.

Chapter Two – Not What I Expected

My new boss was a typical rosy cheeked Dutchman showing the signs that he had spent all his life on the land, working " hands on", running his business. He puffed away on his cigar as he explained that my territory would cover part of Flemish speaking Belgium as well as Southern Holland, and occasional trips to UK. For trips I could use one of the company cars if I wished, or go by train, whichever was the more expedient. The cars were not for personal use, and all kilometers had to be logged in the book. He complimented me on my grasp of his language and said he had never employed a foreigner before, so I better set a good example! My salary would be paid fortnightly and was a bit more than I expected. There was also a generous commission on sales over a targeted amount. That got me in a pleasant mood and as I cycled back to my home I was feeling good. At last I could start to earn some decent money, save up for a holiday maybe or even buy a nice suit. Maybe even buy myself one of those "bromfiets" motorized bicycles?

I stopped by the florist on the way home and bought a potted African Violet for my landlady. Dutch people are very house-proud, and love to fill their houses with plants and flowers. She was very impressed with my gesture of an addition to her already groaning table full of Primula's and various other potted plants. That evening we tucked in to "Erwtensoup" (Pea soup) with chunks of smoked sausage in it, one of my favorite Dutch dishes. The Dutch enjoy hearty and solid winter food that will take them through the freezing and windy winter days without a problem, and I launched myself into this dish with the relish of someone who hadn't seen food for weeks. Miep my landlady was impressed!

The next morning I went to work, the boss Gerrit said he would introduce me to his Sales Manager who would be my direct manager. We went over from his house to the office block just behind the main packing area, turned the corner and just as Gerrit raised a hand to greet the Sales Manager I froze in my tracks. This was the same blond chubby guy that had sat behind me on the boat from England and discussed the diamonds! "Robert, this is Jaap Van Den Bosch" said Gerrit "he is your direct manager and will discuss your first sales trip with you. If you have any problems don't hesitate to come to me though, my door is always open".

I had no idea what I said to Jaap, and he showed no signs of recognizing me, so I just put on a front and started telling him how excited I was to be working for the company. "Now Robert, you have been given the area of parts of Belgium and of course some UK places, but how good is your German? As he asked this he switched to German and expected a reply. My German was not fluent, but I spoke enough to make him realize I could get by. He told me our first trip was to be to Germany, Monday next week we will go to Berlin! My brain must have gone into lockup mode, because he gave me an enquiring look and asked "Is that OK?" "I snapped out of it and lied "Oh yes, fine, sorry I was just thinking how much revision I should be doing on my

German and how I'm going to do it before Monday. I hadn't expected this" I explained. "Easy" said Jaap, "from now we'll just speak German and I'll correct you." I agreed with this. "Now let me take you to the packing floor and explain about these new vacuum packs we are doing for export."

Whilst Jaap was telling me about the product lineup all morning, my head was reeling from what I knew had taken place on the ship two nights before, and how Jaap did not seem to recognise me. He was either very lacking in his observancy skills or genuinely so taken up with his plans that he did not actually put two and two together. Either way I was going to be involved with this guy whether I liked it or not.

When I went home that night I must have appeared very tired as Miep asked the moment I walked in the door if everything was all right. I told her I was just tired from the first day at work and so much to absorb. She had made my favorite sausages with mashed potato and "borekool ", a vegetable that is just delicious! I ate with glee and went straight to bed, feeling very drained from the day and what I had discovered. It made no sense to me what these guys were up to, but I was now going to be involved with them. I decided not to ring my father at this stage, but to find out more about what they were up to and to try and get some proof of what it was they were doing, before starting an unstoppable raising of the alarm. It was certainly not what I had expected on my first day at a new job! I was so tired and drained I slept the sleep of the dead.

The next morning I got to work a half an hour early, to mix with the packing workers and drank coffee making small talk, trying to get under the skin of this company that was so successful in exporting to so many countries around the world. Jaap walked in around 07:30 just as I was getting up to go to the office, and congratulated me on getting in so early and taking the time to get to know people. I explained I thought the heart of any company was its people. They needed to know who was going to represent their hard work in the sales area. I've always been an idealist and I like to see the good side of people that's sometimes been my downfall in that I give people the benefit of the doubt. Sometimes when it's time to get tough, I can't.

The days of the week passed pretty quickly and Friday afternoon at 5:30pm Jaap told me to be at Schiphol Airport at 08:00am on Monday for a 9:30 flight to Berlin. I was quite excited about flying somewhere. I hadn't done much flying, so I spent Saturday getting my clothes ready, then on Saturday evening Miep's daughter Guda said she and her boyfriend were going out to a party, and would I like to come. I thought this was a pretty neat invitation, so accepted, and the three of us walked down Hadleystraat to Begoniastraat. By the time we got there the party was in full swing, there was plenty of drink including the Genever (Dutch gin) but I decided to take it easy and stayed on soft drink most of the night. Guda's boyfriend introduced me to one of his sister's friends, Diny (pronounced Deeny), she lived in Opheliastraat nearby and was on her own, and so we sat and talked about music most of the evening. She was studying music at university and wanted to get into the Concertgebouw orchestra. She explained she loved jazz most of all and we spent most of the evening discussing the keyboard style of Oscar Peterson and Count Basie and how they were both masters in their own way. We both agreed that the piano was such an expressive instrument. I suggested when I got back from my trip we should go to Amsterdam and go and visit some jazz spots, and she liked that idea. So I left the party with a happy glow in my soul, knowing I had not only found an attractive female to take out from time to time but that we had common interests. It had been a nice evening.

On the Sunday, I decided to take the bus into Amsterdam and rekindle my love of this city, walking down Kalverstraat and seeing all the shops that were so familiar from 2 years before. I spotted a "Patat Kraampje". The Dutch have a unique way of serving hot potato chips they serve it in paper cones and with great big dollops of mayonnaise, the taste and texture is something special. As I walked on eating my "Patat met" I really felt like I had come home. I strolled on and came to the "Begijnhof" a small walled square with a Scottish Reformed church in the middle of it. When you walk in, the city's noise totally fades away and you are left in a tranquil little park where you can sit and have a quiet moment. Being winter and cold, I sat in my woolly jumper and heavy winter jacket, enjoying the respite from the wind out in the streets, tucking into my chips. There were not many people about, so the quiet and peace of the square was even more profound. I sat there trying to work out in my mind what to do about this dilemma of the diamonds, and Jaap, and whether or not I should ring my father. I decided that proof of something untoward was required before I could dare to blow the whistle on anything or anybody. So to do nothing was the best course of action at this stage. But

I'd better start keeping some notes so that I could recall details and so on. I walked back towards "Centraal station" down the Damrak and past some of the main tourist areas that were deserted at this time of year. A voice called out "Robert! Here" I looked across the street and there was Jaanus my work mate from two years ago whose father worked in the diamond business! It was good to see a friend and I only then realised that I had been feeling a bit lonely. "Jongen, it's good to see you" he said as he came up towards me, "Have you come back for good?" I replied that I wasn't sure, but I had this job and I loved being back. "Do you have time to come back to the house for a coffee?" he enquired. "Of course" I replied.

We took a number 24 tram to Beethovenstraat to the house he and his family lived in, and there was his father Ton, just as I remembered, puffing away on his Willem cigar. Jaanus informed me that his mother had passed away a year before, and I told him how sorry I was. She had been a great inspiration to me when I had first got to know the family. She was arthritic and suffered terribly through the harsh winters. She had been a survivor of the Second World War and the Germans had not been kind to her on account of her Jewish background. Like many Dutch people of that era, she never forgot or forgave, but she was never a bitter person for all that. Ton was his usual laconic self, sipping on his "Oude Genever". He offered me one and I accepted, the three of us sat there telling each other what had happened in the past two years and sharing some memories. Ton asked me about my job and I told him I was off to Berlin in the morning. He looked hard into my eyes and said "Berlin is a tough place, keep your eyes skinned". I told him I was to be accompanied by my manager, and he seemed to know the ropes. Ton relaxed a little, and said "there's a lot of illegal stones' going through Berlin these days". I must have reacted because he said "just remember the war may be a cold one, but it's still on". I asked him to tell me more about the illegal stones. He smiled and said "well, the story I hear is that the Russians are short of cash, so they are channeling diamonds smuggled out of the mines in South Africa & Sierra Leone via Europe to pay for their KGB activities. "People in the trade have been asked by Interpol to look out for any "over quota" stock roaming about.

I asked him to clarify "over quota" He smiled and went on, "the diamond trade is like a club worldwide everyone in the business knows just about everybody else and what they do. Most shipments of stones are known about, so when extra quantities appear on the scene, questions get asked". "And are questions being asked" I queried. "Right now yes" he replied. "There have been some large quantities of stones stolen and smuggled out of the De Beers mines in South Africa. It appears the workers are bribed to swallow the stones, and walk out after their shift each day with a small undetectable amount inside their bodies. They recover the stones when they get home, and they are collected by an agent for the organization doing the export of the stones. It appears they are being taken overland to North Africa and via cargo ships or airplane to various places in Europe, eventually all brought together in Berlin and taken into East Germany. From there it's anybody's guess what happens, but I would say they get taken straight to Moscow and held for trading or payment of illegal activities anywhere the Russians want". "WOW!" I exclaimed "That is one hell of a story. How do you know all this?" "Like I said" he retorted "the diamond business is a closed shop, anyone trying to muck around with it gets noticed". "So why hasn't Interpol got these guys yet?" I asked. "They have no proof" Ton said with a hint of frustration in his voice. "Also, I suspect the British and American secret services have told them to keep out of the matter as they want to catch the big fish and before they do, find out exactly what else they are up to!" "The diamonds must be used for something?" he queried. I desperately wanted to tell Ton what I had heard on the ship and what I knew, but thought better of it. Maybe when I have more information Ton might be just the person to confide in. But not right now. I said my goodbyes with a promise to come back next Saturday for dinner. I would buy a bottle of duty free cognac on my way back from Berlin for Ton. He loved the stuff but couldn't always afford it.

Chapter Three – A Sense of Dread

Schiphol airport like most airports was very much alive at 08:00 on a Monday morning. Airports never really sleep, they go into an occasional quiet mode, and usually in the middle of the night the hum of cleaning machines cleaning the floors and the occasional announcement is all you hear. But at 08:00 it is busy. The sound of passengers, the PA announcing flights arriving and departing, and the background sound of aircraft engines starting, shutting down and taxiing, it all adds to the excitement of going somewhere.

I took the bus from Aalsmeer to Schiphol East, as the bus stopped directly at the terminal, and I walked into the warm air of the departure hall. Jaap was waiting at the check in counter, and had somebody with him, he waved as I walked towards him and the other man turned and I recognised him as the other thinner dark haired man on the ship. He had a craggy face with hard lines on it as if he had had a lot of stress at some stage in his life. I was not really surprised, that this was the other man from the ship. "This is Kurt Steiglitz" Jaap introduced me to him, and we shook hands.

Kurt explained he worked for the export council which is a government department, that supports Dutch exporters and he had arranged for some diplomatic help in Berlin to try and help exports into East Germany. I expressed surprise that there was any trade allowed with East Germany. Kurt said that certain commodities had trade exemptions.

The bonus for the trip was that as Kurt worked for the government and the trip was partially financed by his dept, we would be flying First Class! I thought that was pretty special and decided to just go with the flow a bit with these guys who obviously enjoyed a good standard of living and knew their way around. We checked in and went to the First Class lounge, where we were offered coffee and cakes the Dutch really know how to make pastries and it's no surprise that they have special shops just devoted to cakes. I sat there with a half an hour to wait before boarding, with my coffee and cake. Jaap went to make a phone call and Kurt wanted to do some paperwork. So I sat and read "Het Parool" a daily Dutch newspaper. There was a story about the latest

Russian attempt to fire a rocket from their base at Baikonur, and how it had failed. NATO radar, at the top of Norway where there is a common border with Russia, had picked up the firing, and reported that the rocket appeared to have been destroyed a few minutes after liftoff. NATO was worried it reported, the Russians might be close to having a longer range inter-continental ballistic missile capable of carrying a nuclear warhead half way round the world. I figured if the rocket didn't work, there wasn't much chance of that being a worry for a while. But it made a good news story.

The flight was called and we walked down the ramp to the tarmac and climbed the front stairs of the KLM Lockheed L188 Electra. We were shown to our very spacious seats and offered a glass of orange juice or champagne. I decide on the juice but Jaap and Kurt got into the bubbles. The huge Allison T56 turbo prop engines started their whine as first one, and then the other three engines were brought to life. The engines stabilized and as the pilot changed pitch control, the blades of the propellers cut into the frosty morning air and we taxied out to the runway. Electra's have a lot of power and a military version is still used today known as the P3 Orion. As the engines were turned to full thrust, I was pushed back into the leather seat, and really felt excited as we leapt into the air and quickly climbed through the grey overcast cloud and burst into the sunshine of the morning. It's a great feeling looking down at the world from an aircraft, and as we climbed, the cloud occasionally parted and allowed me to pick out the land below and catch the occasional reflection of light on the water in canals and the dark brown of the polders below. We climbed to our cruise altitude of

26,000 feet and leveled out. The cabin crew plied us with all manner of edible goodies some of which I sampled and others I refused. I didn't want to appear to the others as one whom over indulged. The captain informed us after about 50 minutes that we were about to enter the Berlin corridor and he would have to descend to 10,000 feet the maximum height allowed in that airspace, and we would be required to keep our seat belts fastened until on the ground at Berlin. The plane began to descend and the turbulence increased as we got down to 10,000 feet, but the bumps weren't that bad. For about 25 minutes we droned on, bouncing around occasionally. I looked out of the window and could make out individual farmhouses below. The plane turned to the left I assumed to begin an approach, but as I looked out again I noticed another aircraft alongside us, a small fighter aircraft. The captain quickly addressed us on the PA, explaining that this was a Russian MIG fighter alongside and that it was the occasional practice of the East German air force to annoy civil aircraft in this way and it was nothing to worry about. I couldn't imagine there was a passenger on board that did not feel some concern about this war bird on our side bristling with weapons. However, after a few minutes it slid behind us and disappeared. The incident gave me a feeling of dread. I don't know why, but it suddenly made me feel ill at ease with the world we were flying into. The plane turned to the right and flaps were deployed, and the rumble of the undercarriage going down was faintly evident from the front of the cabin. We burst out of the cloud, and the first thing I saw was a block of flats going past my left hand window. The approach to Tegel airport is by way of flying past a series of residential blocks and quite disconcerting for a first timer! The plane hovered for a moment as it flared onto the runway. As we taxied to the terminal I could see the snow on the ground that had been piled up in mounds on the side of the taxiways where the snow ploughs had done their job. The cabin crew brought us our coats, and we were told it was minus 4 Celsius outside, a lot colder than Amsterdam.

We walked down the stairs and into the terminal. Immigration formalities only took a few minutes, then on through customs and the baggage claim out into the cold air of Berlin. We took a taxi to the Boulevarde Hotel at Kurfurstendamm, which took about 30 minutes in the traffic, checked ourselves in, and agreed to meet in the lobby for a coffee within 15 minutes. It was about 1pm by now and I was wondering what we would be doing for the rest of the day. I thought so far the day had gone OK. I hadn't put my foot in it at any stage so far, and Kurt seemed a nice enough person. The lobby of the hotel was very comfortable and as I was the first one back down to the lobby I looked around at some of the paintings and prints on the walls. Kurt came up behind me whilst I was looking at one print and startled me. "That is a view of Kurfurstendamm from 100 years ago, quite different now huh?" he said. "Yes, it's certainly changed. most of the old buildings are gone of course?" "Yes bombed in the war" replied Kurt. "My father was a Berliner" he explained, "Oh really?" I asked prompting for more information. "Yes he was sent to work in Holland during the war, he was an objector to the Hitler regime and he was not treated well. That's where he met my mother. They got married and had me, then he was forced to go back to Berlin near the end of the war and was killed by his own countrymen labeled as a traitor. I never really knew him" lamented Kurt. "I am sorry to hear that Kurt" not really knowing what else to say. "It's OK Robert, war makes people behave very differently than they would normally. I have come to terms with those times now, although it was difficult as a child". I suddenly felt genuinely sorry for Kurt, growing up a child not ever knowing his father.

Jaap appeared, and the subject changed to more immediate things. We were going to the department of trade to try and agree on some quotas that had been nominally set for importations of retail pre-packed seeds from Holland. Kurt explained he was going to try and increase the quotas as it was not really economic to ship the quantities that had been set. We took a cab to a large grey building on Grunewaldstrasse, and announced our presence to the receptionist who asked us to take a seat. After a few minutes' two men appeared, one young man, who told us he was Friedrich and an older, I assumed more senior man called Mikael. Mikael welcomed us and ushered us into a boardroom, where there was a crackling fire in the fireplace, and the smell of hot fresh coffee greeted our senses. "Gentlemen please make yourself comfortable, you have had a long journey today" said Mikael. "And one not without incident I hear?" Jaap asked what he was referring to, and Mikael explained it had been on the news that an East German fighter had intercepted a KLM aircraft. "But the captain said that often happens" said Jaap, "well, not that often that it doesn't make the news" smiled Mikael.

Coffee was brought to us at the table and we started discussing the quota's and the problem of the size of each shipment being restricted. Friedrich and Mikael explained they did not want the local market to be flooded with imports as there were some local suppliers who felt they would lose their share of the market. Jaap asked how many local suppliers there were and Friedrich said there only two, very influential people and they did not want them to feel threatened by imports being unrestricted. Jaap also explained it would be uneconomic to ship in the quantities suggested and that maybe we would not be able to supply the Berlin market at all. This caused a silence in the room. Clearly Friedrich and Mikael did not like this idea either. Then Jaap turned to me and said "Robert you are the new boy on the block, what would you do?" I had been thinking this through and actually did have an idea, but it was a bit outside the square. "Well these local suppliers as I understand it are wholesalers and have some shops of their own and also supply to other retailers, right?" I asked. "That is correct" said Mikael. "Well instead of us going to the retailers direct, what about we talk to these two companies with a view to supplying them wholesale exclusively and they sell our products which are much higher quality than they currently have, to the retailers themselves? That way they get a margin out of it and are less likely to oppose a quota, because they stand to sell more anyway". Mikael and Friedrich both smiled and Mikael said "this is a good concept, I'm sure we can talk to these people and make it work". I decided to push the point. "What about we try and meet with them tomorrow and get an agreement?" Friedrich said he thought that was possible and would ring us at the hotel later to confirm this, then stood up as if to conclude the meeting. Jaap and Kurt nodded to me and we left the room and said our goodbyes in the foyer of the building. The meeting had taken less than 30 minutes.

We got into a cab and so far neither Kurt nor Jaap had said anything to me. I had that feeling of dread again that I had gone completely overboard on this. Then as the cab pulled away both Kurt and Jaap turned to me with a broad grin and Kurt said "that's the best piece of negotiating I've seen for years!" Jaap retorted "that was a master stroke!" I felt relieved to say the least. "You realize what you have done Robert?" said Kurt. "Not exactly" I replied. "Well you have just set the foundations of our product having unlimited access to this market" he said with a gleam in his eye. "If these guys agree to this then the product they will be getting will be far superior to anything they have seen before and we'll corner the best part of the market with them making a poultice out of it as well! I replied "Well, let's see if we can get them to agree first".

We got back to our hotel and there was a message from Mikael. He had spoken to both suppliers and in principle they liked the idea, and would we meet again at their office at 10am tomorrow for a meeting with them all? Jaap rang back and confirmed. He told me that he and Kurt had a private meeting that evening with some old friends of Kurt and apologized for not being able to include me, but that tomorrow night we would go out and celebrate if the deal was agreed to. I said that was fine, obviously they did not know I would be coming when the trip was first planned, so I would be happy to have dinner at the hotel and get an early night. I had other plans though.

I went to my room and relaxed for an hour thinking over the day, and what had unfolded. If I had scored a few points in their eyes then that was good. they might trust me and not suspect that I knew they were up to something. Jaap was in the room next to me and about an hour later I heard his door close and gave him about 40 seconds before I followed. I took the stairs however not the lift, as I got to the lower level I spotted he and Kurt going out the front foyer door, they walked down the street and turned into Joachimstalerstrasse, passing the orthodox synagogue. They turned into the Art Hotel Sokat, a hotel frequented by artists. The hotel itself is decorated with contemporary art.

I saw them go into the restaurant and meet with another two men, one had a long black beard wearing a dark suit, and the other was of middle eastern appearance and wore grey trousers with a black leather jacket. They sat down to order drinks, and look at the menu. I decided to go on down the street and noticed there was a small café on the other side of the road diagonally across from the hotel. I walked in and selected a table near the window and behind a pillar, this was an excellent vantage point. I could see the Sokat entrance from here so would see if they left. I ordered a glass of red wine, and looked at the menu glancing across the street every minute or so. I ordered a plate of goulash and it was served quickly and came with a serving of crusty dark rye bread that was just wonderful.

As I was tucking in to my goulash and about half way through it, there was a huge orange flash from across the road at Sokat. A millisecond later a thunderous roar ripped my eardrums apart and the entire plate glass window of the café imploded, scattering glass in all directions. As the explosion subsided, it was replaced by the screams and cries of people in great pain. I checked myself and realized that because of the pillar just behind me at the window I had been shielded from the blast to a great degree, and apart from a small cut on my hand, I was miraculously intact.

I looked around the now shattered café, and saw one man with half his face blown away. He had staggered in from the street. Most people in the café had not sustained great injuries, so with the sound of wailing sirens in the distance, I ventured out into the street to see what can be only described as a battle zone. The entire front of the Sokat had been blown in, and there was a smoldering wreck of what was once a car in front of the building. This had obviously been the source of the explosion. The thought that it might have been a bomb did not dawn on me until a man rushed up to me and said in a panicked voice "there may be more bombs, be careful!" It then occurred to me that what I had witnessed was no accident. Then I suddenly thought, my god Jaap and Kurt are in there! I rushed over and saw people covered in blood struggling out of what was the front of the hotel but was now a heap of rubble. I heard from behind me a familiar voice, "Robert, it's Jaap I'm over here, I looked behind me and there he was bleeding from the face but OK otherwise. "I heard the explosion, and came to see what was going on" I said trying to make out I had come from the hotel we were staying at. "Are you all right? Where's Kurt?" I queried. "He's still in there I think" Jaap stammered. We went up to the steps of the hotel. it was shocking to hear the cries of trapped people. We tried moving some of the large chunks of concrete that had fallen from the façade of the building. We pulled a woman out from under one piece, but she was dead. The ambulances had now arrived as well as the fire brigade and a host of police. It was chaotic but the police got it under control fairly quickly. We saw Kurt being carried out on a stretcher by ambulance personnel and rushed over to him, "We think he has no more than a broken arm and concussion" said one of the ambulance crew. "Hop in with us and we'll take him to the hospital"

We lurched through the streets with sirens wailing and arrived at the Franziskuskrankenhaus within minutes. "How did you know we were there?" asked Jaap as we waited for someone to inform us about Kurt. "Hmm? Oh I didn't, I just had something to eat and decided to go for a walk before going to bed, and turned the corner as the explosion had just happened" I explained. "Oh, I see" said Jaap. He went to a phone to make a call and I overheard him telling someone about the incident. He told them they would have to wait a while now until the situation was clarified. He would wait for instructions he told the person at the other end. We waited until just after midnight and Kurt appeared with his arm in a sling and looking bruised but OK, we arranged for transport back to our hotel and were relieved to get back there. We sat and had a cognac together, as Kurt said he needed a stiff drink before sleep, we were all drained and said our goodnights to each other and went to our rooms. I had a shower before falling into bed and a very deep sleep.

The first thing I remember is the alarm going off at 7am and decided to roll over and get another half hour before realizing we had agreed to meet at 8am for breakfast. "What a day that was!" greeted Kurt. "Certainly don't want too many of those" I replied. "How are you feeling?" I enquired. "Not too bad actually" he said. Jaap appeared a few minutes later. He was actually looking worse than Kurt, I suspect he had not slept well.

"What do you two think that was all about last night "I asked of them. "I honestly don't know" said Jaap, and Kurt nodded "according to the newspaper this morning it was some extremist group trying to prove a point". But I knew from the look in their eyes they were both lying. "They certainly must have had a lot of explosives to do that much damage" I added. Kurt said "I would say they must have loaded that car with a boot full of explosives and remotely set it off". "Can that be done?" I asked, trying to get them to say what they knew. "Sure it can, you just need a radio device with a trigger activated by a certain frequency" said Jaap, "my father was in the ordnance during the war and they had such devices then". Well, they weren't going to let me in on the real story so I decided to drop this tack and wait for them to make a mistake. I could see from their attitude they were frightened.

After breakfast we went back to our rooms and agreed to meet in the foyer at 9:30am to take a cab to Grunewaldstrasse. I decided to make some notes about what had happened. As I was doing this I heard Jaap's door open, obviously Kurt had decided they needed to talk, because I heard raised voices from Jaap's room. Using the old glass against the wall technique I listened in to their conversation. Kurt said he thought they were very lucky to have got away alive from the incident. "It just shows how serious they are" said Jaap. "I think we arrange to hand over the diamonds this afternoon and ask no more questions. We don't want another incident" warned Kurt. "Where exactly do the stones go from here?" asked Jaap . "It's none of our business" replied Kurt. "All we want is the money and we better not ask for more. That's exactly why we were warned last night, if that was a warning I don't want them to get serious".

"So it's agreed then, we do this drop and then the last one in Hamburg in two weeks time, then we get our money, no sooner "said Kurt. I deduced from this conversation that they had tried to screw money out of whoever they were supplying, earlier than had been agreed upon, and last night's debacle was a way of saying wait until the deal is fully complete. Whoever was on the other side was deadly serious, and didn't care if anyone innocent or otherwise got in the way.

Chapter Four – The Deal Is Done

We walked into the Grunewaldstrasse offices and were greeted by the smiling faces of Mikael and Friedrich. They in turn introduced us to Hubert and Oskar who were the principles of the two supplier companies. They obviously knew each other well, as they chatted between themselves as they went into the boardroom. "Well, gentlemen Oskar and I have discussed your interesting plan of being your exclusive suppliers to the retail businesses here, and think it is an excellent idea. The reputation of your products is well known, so, we propose an initial order of 6 container loads of mixed prepacks, we will give you a cheque for 10% of the order as soon as you confirm pricing. Which we assume will be the usual 50% of recommended retail, we will add 20% as our margin, and that way the retailers will get the 30% and those retail outlets we own will do even better". Jaap nodded his agreeance to this and added." We will send you some free samples of all of our pre-packs within the next 48 hours and you can select what proportion of the various types you want". Oskar and Hubert were pleased with this suggestion. The trade executive Mikael had already drawn up a contract of understanding which we all signed and witnessed. The deal was done! It all seemed so easy I thought, much too easy!

As we got into our cab back to the hotel Kurt congratulated me on a job well done and added, "we will celebrate tonight, because this deal will be worth many millions of guilders over the coming year or so. Tomorrow we will fly back to Amsterdam". I felt good about what had happened but also suspicious, it was all too easy and I felt I was being drawn in to something without knowing what it was. I resolved to talk to Ton on the weekend about the whole story, he was to be my mentor in this matter.

When I got back to the hotel Jaap advised he and Kurt had one more appointment to attend by themselves and that I should relax for the afternoon and meet them at 7:00pm for drinks before dinner. Jaap said he had to meet with a police official in half an hour before they went out, to make a written statement and after he would require me to make a statement also. I told him to give me a ring in my room and I'd be happy tell what I had seen. The thought then occurred to me whether I should tell the police that I had been in the café or the version I had told Jaap and Kurt about coming from the hotel for a walk and stumbling into the incident. I decided to tell the police the real story as I might be asked more questions and people might say they had seen me in the café.

The phone rang in my room about 2:30pm. Jaap asked me to come down and make the statement. To my relief when I got there Jaap made his apologies about going to the other meeting, so it was just me and the detective, he said his name was Ivan and that he was from the special incident unit. He asked where I was when the explosion occurred, and I said in the café across the street from the Sokat. He asked why I was there and I said I just decided to take a walk and decided to stop for a coffee. "According to the Restaurant owner you ordered a meal, goulash I believe?" Ivan had done his homework. "Oh yes, when I walked in and smelled the good food, I decided to eat, I had eaten a snack earlier, but was still hungry so ordered that and a glass of red wine" I bluffed. So what happened? Asked Ivan. "Well, just as I got my goulash and had eaten about half of it, there was this huge explosion and fireball from across the street. The window of the restaurant imploded in, and shards of glass went everywhere and because I was behind a pillar I was lucky to just have a few scratches". "Yes, you were fortunate" agreed Ivan, "If that pillar had not been in the way you would probably be dead". He stated coldly. "So, you did not see exactly what caused the explosion?" "No" I replied "But I assumed the car outside the hotel was where the bomb or whatever caused the explosion, was located because when I went across from the café, the car was still burning and was totally wrecked." "In our business we never assume Mr Ellis" He cautioned. "Your assumption is likely correct, but forensic will confirm all that in due course". He added. "Now, tell me what happened when you went over to the hotel?" "Well, I saw a lot of dust in the air and rubble lying about, there were people screaming and crying for help. But it would have been dangerous to go into the wreckage I thought, so I just helped those that came out, until more help arrived. Oh, and yes, there was a man who came towards me as I came out of the café yelling to be careful there might be more bombs" "Oh!" queried Ivan "Can you remember what he looked like"? "He was about 5feet 9ins tall. Sorry I don't know that in meters, it comes from my English education! He was wearing a dark blue anorak, with jeans and those exercise shoes with white laces. He spoke German in an accent maybe East European, Hungary or Poland maybe?" " Piotr Chevanyah" said Ivan. "I'm sorry, I don't understand" I queried. "Piotr Chevanyah, is a prime suspect in this and other terrorist incidents around Europe in the past 2 years. He is part of a cell of people who wish to see East Germany given back to the west and he always appears at the scene afterwards, presumably to admire his handiwork" said Ivan. "You have done well my friend! You are the only person to positively identify this man" Ivan paused and looked to the ceiling. "We better arrange for some protection for you for the remainder of your stay here, and we may need you to come back later to help our enquiries." "One thing puzzles me" I queried. "If they want East Germany given back to the west, why bomb in the western part of Berlin?" Ivan explained. "They think that by causing harm and promoting fear on both sides they will force someone's hand, they have done this sort of thing on the other side too. They are desperate people" Ivan said he had to go, but may need to talk again tomorrow before I left Berlin. "Oh one last question Mr Ellis, did you know your colleagues were in the hotel before Jaap came out?" "No, I didn't, I was surprised to see them" I lied. "OK, thank you for your help" said Ivan as he turned and left.

I went back to my room to rest for a few hours, until my alarm rang at 5:30pm. I had decided to wake with enough time to get myself ready for a night out on the town, with my new colleagues, albeit that I trusted them about as far as one can throw a battleship. I had a shower and laid on the bed listening to the 6:00pm news on the radio. It was full of the news of the bombing from last night. There were four people dead. The first death toll I had heard of. It seems three had died instantly and one of injuries at the hospital later. I shuddered, as I thought that I could have been one of those statistics. They were quoting sources in the police force as saying it was an extremist terrorist group that was to blame. It's only when you are caught up in such an extraordinary situation as this, you start to question how desperate people can get to achieve their goals. I had to admit I was scared that I was now involved in all this.

I dressed and went down to the bar to have a quiet drink before meeting the others, but Jaap was already there, sipping on a Beck's beer. I joined him and ordered the same. I felt thirsty. We sat and made small talk about how we would get the samples shipped as soon as we got back in the morning. He told me he had rung Gerritt earlier to tell him what a star I had been, and that Gerritt wanted to take me out to dinner when we got back to say thanks. I was pleased I had got off to a flying start. I liked Gerritt and wanted to be a part of the team. Kurt joined us and said he had asked reception to get us a taxi. I asked where we were going and was told it was surprise. The taxi took us on a similar route that we had taken to Grunewaldstrasse earlier in the day, but turned into Akazienstrasse and pulled up outside Gottlob restaurant. It was an impressive frontage to the premises as we walked in Kurt was greeted in first name terms by the maitre d'hôtel. We were shown to a table in a quiet corner. The menu was extensive and we needed time to choose carefully, so Kurt had already arranged for a bottle of Krug 1954 to be chilled and waiting for us. We raised our glasses. "To a highly successful and certainly action filled trip" said Jaap. Kurt still had his right arm in a sling so raised his glass with his left and said "You have raised the stakes my friend". I pondered this for a moment, and asked "what do you mean"? "The Berlin market has never been cracked before by your company and you managed to do it on your first trip! That must be a sales record?" Jaap responded "You may not know of this yet but the sales team has a private competition as to who can make the maximum sales effort through the year. Gerritt rewards them with a holiday fully paid by the company. I would say you are well on the way to making the top sales person for the year with this effort" "Well, I really wouldn't have done it without the input from you Kurt and the help from Jaap". I responded. It was nevertheless comforting to know I had the confidence of the two of them.

I chose the Roast Quail to start with and a Tournedo steak rare, with fresh vegetables and béarnaise sauce for main course. We had an excellent Chateau Lafite 1957 to accompany, and continued with the cheese board to finish with. Coffee and Armagnac rounded off a magnificent meal. What a life I considered. Here I am nearly 18 years old living the high life in Berlin! My father would be extremely jealous when I told him. Then I suddenly remembered I had not written or told my father or mother anything since I left UK. They would be wondering what on earth I was up to. I resolved to write a letter to them on the plane tomorrow. "This has been a very memorable evening gentlemen, thank you". I told them both. They both responded that it was a pleasure to be working with me. We had another round of coffee's and Armagnac's and then took a taxi back to our hotel, where we quickly agreed to meet around 9:00am for breakfast, our flight was not till midday, so we had plenty of time. I slept well that night.

Chapter Five - "Curiouser & Curiousor" said Alice

Tegel airport has a relatively small terminal and the departure hall was crowded with people that morning. There had been fog earlier and many flights were delayed, causing pandemonium for those waiting for aircraft that had not arrived. After check in, I went straight to the duty free shop and bought a bottle of Remy Martin VSOP for Ton. Our flight, which was to be operated by an incoming aircraft from Amsterdam, was not delayed yet, but I imagined with such a backlog of passengers that some delay would be inevitable due to air traffic restrictions if nothing else. It was therefore a relief to escape to the relative calm of the First Class lounge with Jaap and Kurt and have a comfortable seat, a coffee, and read the papers, something which I had not done much of in the past week. There was a copy of the London Daily Telegraph available, so I grabbed it quickly and read it ravenously. The headlines were discussing the coming UK elections and that did not interest me much, but at the foot of the front page was a story that grabbed my attention, there was a brewing spy scandal in Westminster. It appears the press had got hold of rumors of a double agent working for the Russians in the highest department of MI5, and whilst they were keen to keep it out of the press someone had blown the whistle. The story discussed the possibility that the Russians might have got hold of some very secret documents relating to defence projects under way. It outlined how embarrassing it would be for the British, to have to explain to the Americans, that some of their data may also have fallen into undesirable hands. What a mess! I thought. Dear old Whitehall would be buzzing with gossip. My father often said that security was good in his department, but as soon as Whitehall got involved there was always a "stuff up" somewhere to make life difficult. It was common knowledge that in these cold war days the British and allies would try anything including double agents to get secrets from the Russians, so I guess this was an example of it working both ways. I pondered as to what information the Russians might be gloating over right now.

"Would you like another coffee sir?" asked the waiter, "Oh, yes please, thank you" I had got so in to the story in the paper I had forgotten where I was, so the waiter made me jump. I looked across at Kurt, he was talking to a man I hadn't seen before, and gesticulating quite aggressively with his hands, suddenly the man pulled a gun and yelled "Get back, or I'll shoot" people gasped in horror. A policeman appeared at the door that led out the departure gates right behind the man. Without any fuss and not a word, he drew his pistol and shot the man in the back, he fell to the ground dead. His feet rattled against the floor and the last of his nerve energy expended itself in a useless attempt to move his legs. Some primeval instinct embedded in his brain. Blood trickled from the dead man's ear as he lay there. The people in the lounge stood transfixed in horrified silence, I was still seated and could scarcely believe what I had seen. Kurt came over to me and I asked him what on earth that was about. He said I shouldn't worry, the man had mistaken him for someone else and when he had tried to identify himself the man produced the gun. I didn't believe a word of what he told me, but how could I prove otherwise? The policeman came over to us and asked Kurt if he would accompany him to his office downstairs to make a statement and that it should not delay him long as it was clearly a case of mistaken identity. By this time ambulance crews had arrived and were preparing to cover the body. Other police started clearing the lounge area. Airline staff ushered as all to another lounge and some people were treated for shock. Jaap in the meantime had gone to do some shopping and knew nothing of what had happened. So when he got to the lounge and was redirected to where we had been taken, he rushed up to me quite flustered "What on earth has happened?" he asked. I explained what had taken place, and he went quite pale. I gave him a glass of water. "What exactly is going on here?" I demanded. "First you two are in a bombing attempt, then this, are they connected? " "I don't think so" said Jaap. I did not believe him and my eyes must have told him so as he leant on my shoulder and said "When we get back to Amsterdam, I'll fill you in on all of this, it's only fair." I was relieved if nothing else that my imagination was not playing tricks on me. I wondered what he would tell me. Certainly not the truth I thought.

Kurt came back and explained the police did not want to see him again and it was clearly a deranged person that had tried to shoot him and they were satisfied with that. I asked him if his diplomatic status helped him in this sort of situation and he said it helped to identify him only to police as someone who had diplomatic privileges but it did not protect him from the laws of the land. He seemed very disturbed, but not about the fact that he had nearly been shot. He looked at Jaap and said "we better go to the plane, the flight has just been called" We went out of the lounge to the gate, where we were escorted by two policemen to the foot of the front stairs of the Electra. I was very relieved to sink in to the leather seat and gladly accepted the glass of champagne that was offered. The cool effect on my throat as the bubbles dispersed and the yeasty smell of the champagne helped to settle my nerves. I suddenly realized I had suffered some degree of shock about what had taken place before me in the past few days and the knowledge that these guys did not seem to be very disturbed about it. They seemed more worried about their plans being disrupted than the human lives that had been lost. I never heard them even comment further on the disaster at the Hotel Sokat.

The KLM Electra taxied out to the runway and after a short wait whilst a BEA Vanguard took off ahead of us, our plane moved into position and at full throttle hurtled down the runway and projected itself into the sky. I love that moment of transition from a mass of ground based hurtling metal, into a flying machine that seems so much more at home once it departs the runway. I mused that the aircraft that had taken off ahead of us was probably bound for London Heathrow and what I wouldn't give to be on that plane right now. Home seemed a long way away and I realized it had only been 14 days since I had got on board the boat at Harwich. Such a lot had happened. I decided that tonight when I got back to Aalsmeer, I would ring Ton and confirm our

Saturday dinner and tell him I wanted to talk about some serious matters first.

The flight back to Amsterdam was uneventful. I tucked into the hot lunch that was served. Fine cuts of lamb, just pink and served with a julienne of vegetables. A few glasses of Chateau Haut Brion to wash it down. Coffee and I even had a cognac with it. I felt slightly inebriated when we started our descent into Schiphol but it also made me feel confident that things would sort themselves out. Amazing how a few drinks can give you a different view on the way matters are!

When we got through customs, Jaap said he was going to grab a taxi with Kurt and drop him off at his home on the way, and I should take a taxi back to Aalsmeer and he would catch up with me at the office in the morning. I was pleased at the prospect of being out of sight of these two and away from their inherent danger. I was glad that tomorrow was Friday and I would have a weekend to recover and catch up with Jaanus and Ton on Saturday. As we cleared customs and came out into the arrivals hall Kurt and Jaap were met by a man, who Kurt obviously knew, but was not expecting. The man did not introduce himself to me but just said there was a car waiting and they made a hurried departure with Jaap saying to me "see you in the morning". I saw them get into the black Mercedes and the car quickly sped off into the traffic. I went to a taxi, and as I was putting my suitcase into the boot, I realized I had Jaap's briefcase. It had got mixed up with my bags somehow. It seemed very light, almost empty, but I kept hold of it and took it into the cab with my own briefcase. I gave the driver instructions how to get to Hadleystraat, and wondered what could possibly be in the briefcase, was it diamonds, money? Why was it so light? I tried the lock but it was not unlocked and I wasn't going to try and tamper with it, certainly not in the back of a taxi!

It gets dark very early in November in Holland, and by the time I got home it was 4:30pm and nearly dark. Miep my landlady was glad to see me home and made me a cup of coffee while I told her some of the detail about the success I had on the trip. I left out all the stuff that had happened at the Sokat and the airport. I went up to my room and looked at the briefcase, I shook it and nothing rattled or moved inside it seemed as though it was empty. I turned it upside down and the base was solid leather with four brass studs, one in each corner. For some reason I tried turning one of the studs and it turned anti clockwise, and started to unscrew. I unscrewed all four and the base came away revealing a compartment about 1in deep along the entire base of the briefcase. It was empty but it was obvious that this had been used to conceal diamonds or money as it would not have held anything bulky. No wonder Jaap had it at his feet on the boat! I screwed the base back on and wiped the brass studs to remove any finger marks I may have left. I was not going to leave anything to chance. How curious though that Jaap had left this case accidentally with me, or was it deliberate? "Curiouser and curiouser said Alice" I thought to myself, stealing a Lewis Carrol line.

Chapter 6 – What Is Going On Here?

I got to work around 7:30 that morning. Jaap was already there. I gave him back his briefcase and he showed no surprise except to thank me for bringing it in. He explained it was empty, as he had put all his papers in his main suitcase for the flight home. I made a cup of coffee for us both and decided now was the time to confront him. "Jaap just what is going on here?" I questioned vigorously. All of my senses told me I was not going to hear the truth, but a version that he wanted me to believe. I resolved to go along with his charade. "Robert, Kurt and I are involved in a business that is not pretty, as a result of Kurt's diplomatic connections he has become a target for blackmail. It is on a highly political level and when he got stuck in the position of having nowhere to turn, he came to me as an old school friend for help". Maybe I was going to hear the truth after all I pondered. Jaap continued, "as a result of his father being killed and his mother dead with no other family around, Kurt is a loner, and he has now become involved in smuggling diamonds as a result of some silly mistakes he made a few years ago in Germany. He compromised himself with a prostitute, and she was used by a smuggling ring. As a result photos were produced and Kurt was told they would be sent to his superiors if he didn't comply. He stupidly thought that if he went to the police he would still lose his job anyway, and so went along with these people. They pay him, but keep upping the stakes and now I have become implicated too. Let me show you something". Jaap grabbed the briefcase I had brought back to him. "I deliberately left this with you last night because I didn't know if the people picking us up were hostile or not". He unscrewed the base of the briefcase and showed me the compartment I had already discovered. Then he pushed a small catch in the top of the hidden base that I had not noticed last night, a flap in the false base appeared and inside was a small linen pouch. He took it out and pulled the drawstring free and out fell around 30 small diamonds. "These are worth around half a million guilders" said Jaap.

I gasped. I had been carrying around a small fortune in stones! "Blue white and baguette cut" I stammered. "Very good Robert" exclaimed Jaap . "You know a bit about stones huh?" he questioned. "Well, I used to work with a guy whose father was in the business". That was a stupid thing to reveal, I thought to myself but it was too late. "I see, well anyway Kurt is now so up to his neck in this and me too, that we can't really go back without putting ourselves in real trouble". "I am telling you this so that you understand why all that mess happened in Berlin. They were trying to kill us" Jaap said coldly. "They wanted it to look like a political killing but it's really about money". "Why do they need the diamonds?" I questioned. "Diamonds are an international currency, not numbered, very difficult to trace unlike paper money". He explained. "Does the boss know about all this?" I asked. "No, he knows nothing" said Jaap. "Then why are you telling me all this?" I queried. Jaap went on "we had to tell you because you had become so suspicious and we didn't want you to go to the police" We will of course make it worth your while to keep quiet about it" He reassured. "What do you mean?" I gasped. "Well, for your silence in the matter we will pay you let's say a bit of a bonus. Let's say, you take these diamonds, and forget it ever happened?" I must have looked shocked, because he went on "there will be more in it for you later, if you want to help us" he stated. I don't know what possessed me, but I decided to go along with it, not for the diamonds, but to find out more about what they were up to, I did not believe this was the full story. "OK, Jaap, I'm in!" I blurted. "Good man" he exclaimed. He handed me the small pouch and told me to put them somewhere safe. I had no idea where I would keep them, but I would certainly be taking them to Ton's place tomorrow night.

For the rest of the day I hardly remember what I did. I recall going through some sales figures with Jaap, and Gerritt coming to the office to congratulate me on the contract. I had nearly forgotten the whole thing with all this going on. He asked us to stay for drinks after work to celebrate with all the staff. At 5:30pm we all gathered in the packing shed with the staff and had beers and "borreltjes", the Dutch gin flowed generously. The men puffed on their cigars and I figured this was the real meaning of "gezellig", the dictionary translates this word into English as "cosy", but it 's more than that, it's that warm, belonging, feeling you get when you are comfortable with the place and the people around you.

Gerritt made a small speech to congratulate me on my good work and told the staff there would be plenty of work from this contract. They all seemed pretty pleased and we finished the week off with a lot of happy faces leaving work to enjoy their weekend. Gerritt said he would like to invite me to dinner with him and his wife on Monday evening as a thank you gesture, I accepted graciously. But I felt I had less enjoyable and more serious matters to attend to before Monday rolled around. I cycled home and felt very tired when I got there, Miep had cooked her usual hearty meal. Tonight it was pork chops with cabbage and potatoes. We sat around the fire later watching TV an old movie "Sun Valley Serenade" with the Glen Miller band supplying plenty of schmaltzy music. I needed an escape tonight and this was good. Before going to bed I walked down the street to call Ton and confirm tomorrow night's dinner, on the way I met Diny, she was walking the family poodle. She asked if I had enjoyed my trip, I told her it had been successful and I had got a contract out of it, she seemed impressed. She asked if I was doing anything tomorrow night as there was a party at her friends place. I explained I was just on my way to ring Ton to confirm my invitation for dinner, and suggested she might want to come with me, she said that would be nice. I rang Ton and told him there would be two of us and he said he would be pleased to meet my new friend. I went back home and tumbled into bed, I must have been asleep before my head hit the pillow.

It was 10am before I woke, I hurriedly shaved and showered and went downstairs, Miep explained she didn't want to wake me as it didn't matter to her and I obviously needed the sleep. I had lots of hot coffee and those Dutch egg biscuits with jam on them. It was a good start to the day. I told Miep I would be out tonight and would not be back till late, when I told her I was going with Diny she raised her eyebrows and said "You are a fast worker!" I did some washing and by the time I had finished it was 1pm, so I went round to Diny's house to see if she was home and she was there playing some records. I said maybe we should go into Amsterdam and walk around the shops, she thought that was a great idea. We went back to my place to pick up the cognac for Ton and I put the diamonds in my pocket, I had hidden them under the bed in my briefcase as there was nowhere else to put them that was secure. We took the bus into Amsterdam and spent the rest of the afternoon looking around the shops. We went into C&A Kloppenburg department store and Diny looked at clothes for a while, the thought crossed my mind that with the stones in my pocket I could just about buy her everything in the store! I wondered how I could tell Ton about what had happened without Diny hearing our conversation, maybe it wasn't such a good idea to have invited her after all. But I figured if she got to hear the story, so what?

We took the tram to Ton's place about 6pm and bought a nice bottle of red wine at the liquor store just down the street, a nice Bordeaux, Ton liked a good red. When we arrived he and Jaanus made a big fuss of Diny and she lapped it up. I said I needed to talk to Ton about some business I had stumbled upon that might interest him, he asked Diny and Jaanus to excuse us for a while and they poured themselves another drink and started talking about music, I had forgotten Jaanus was a good piano player. We went into Ton's study and I took out the linen pouch and emptied the stones onto his leather topped desk. He gasped, "Where the hell did you get those?" he demanded. "They are fine looking stones" He took out his eyeglass to study individual stones. "These were cut by Verhoeven in Antwerp!" How do you know that? " I questioned. "Each polisher and cutter leaves his mark or style of cut on stones, but you have to know what you are looking for", he explained. I started to tell him the story and after about half an hour had told him most of what I knew. "There is more to this than you know my friend". "I guessed there probably is" I stated. "I will arrange for us to meet with a friend of mine who is in the security services, tomorrow", He carried on.

"But that's Sunday" I protested. "It's too urgent to wait" He said firmly. "Now let's pay attention to your lady friend and enjoy dinner!" We came out of his study and he had already put the stones in his safe, I felt re-assured that Ton knew what to do about all this.

The dinner was great, Jaanus had cooked a beef roast and it was very good. Ton had made his legendary Crème Brulee' for dessert. We had a great evening and as we walked to the tram stop Diny grabbed my arm and said what lovely friends I had. Her hair glowed in the lights at the tram stop, highlighting her pretty face, and I wanted to give her a kiss, but couldn't find the courage. She smiled at me and she knew what I was thinking, the tram came and we got on board, she snuggled up close to me on the seat and gave me a peck on the cheek and thanked me for a lovely evening out. I told her the pleasure was entirely mine and I would like to take her out more, she said that was a great idea and that she would look forward to the next time. I thought I would try and get some tickets for a concert of some kind for the coming week, and invite her to that as a surprise. We talked about music most of the way home and she didn't even ask about what business Ton and I had discussed. I liked this girl, she was mature and sensible. I escorted her to her door and although I would have liked to have given her a goodnight kiss, decided it was not appropriate on a first date. As I walked home I had a good feeling about Diny.

Sunday morning, I woke about 9:00am and had breakfast with lots of coffee. At around 10:00am a large silver Mercedes drew up outside the house and Ton got out and knocked on the door, I opened it and asked him in, but he said no, and would I be good enough to go with him straight away? I explained to Miep that Ton was a friend and I would be back later. I got into the car and Ton introduced me to the other occupant, Ralph Philips was his name from the British Embassy in Rotterdam. Ralph said we would be going direct to his office and that all would be explained once we were there. I wondered what on earth was going on. It took about 50 minutes to get there and hardly a word was said the entire journey. We entered a large grey building and descended into the car park. I was ushered into a lift and we emerged into a corridor, where Ralph invited us in to an office that was in the very corner of the building with a large window overlooking the port of Rotterdam. The Euro tower was clearly visible, who ever Ralph was, he was a fairly senior civil servant, as my father had often explained that corner offices and large ones at that, were only afforded to those of high rank and it was a very highly coveted perk of office.

"Mr Ellis, my name is not really Ralph and who I work for is more important for you to know than my identity as an individual, Her Majesty's government have empowered my department to protect and defend information that is important to the NATO alliance and all United Kingdom's allies. Ton your friend here is a valued agent of my department and has helped us over the years to keep us informed of many important matters. I must inform you that as of now you are subject to the National Secrets Act and anything said or implied to you today must never be divulged to anyone. Do you understand? "I replied with a nod and a muffled "Yes". I was totally out of my depth here, and had no idea what was going on. A door opened at the other end of the room and to my total shock, in walked my father!! "Hello Robert, you

really have got yourself in deep in this one my boy!"
"Dad! What is this all about?" I exclaimed. Ralph
interjected. " Don't worry Mr Ellis, we will tell you all you
need to know over the coming hour or so, just pay
attention and you may find you are able to help your
country and your father more than you may think"

"Mr Ellis, the people you have accompanied to Berlin in
the past week are known agents in the pay of the
Russian Government, forget anything they may have told
you, because they want to manipulate you as an
apparently innocent party in their midst. What they are
up to, is potentially devastating to the western alliance,
in that they are trying to fund the theft of information
pertaining to work of a highly secret nature being
undertaken by Her Majesty's governments department
of which your father is a member". Ralph looked to my
father, as if to hand over the conversation to him. My
Father went on "Robert, you may remember seeing the
Blue Streak folder in my office one day when you
accidentally came in without knocking?" "Yes" I replied
"And Jaap and Kurt were talking about it on the boat"
"Yes we know" said my father. "What you don't know
and I'm about to explain, is that this project is a missile
called an Intercontinental Ballistic Missile that could,
once it is completed, carry nuclear warheads half way
round the world. The Russians are developing something
similar, but their guidance technology is not as good as
ours, and we believe they want to get their hands on the
plans. The first test firing is at Woomera in a month or
so in South Australia and once we know the technology
works they will be even more desperate to get their
hands on it."

"So where do Jaap and Kurt come into all this? " I questioned. Ralph interjected, "The Russians and the KGB are basically broke, and they have no funds to speak of. What Jaap and Kurt are doing is to collect from various points around Europe, diamonds stolen from the African mines. They will use them to pay informers in the British Government departments for copies of papers they will steal. Diamonds are a much better form of payment than any currency as Ton has already explained to you. We know who most of the informers are, and are watching them, but we want to catch the big fish here as well, there are higher levels of informers and possibly some government ministers in on this. And we need to catch every one of them. The Americans are concerned that by sharing information with us their secrets are also in jeopardy and the entire NATO alliance could be undermined if that happens."

"What about the bombing in Berlin?" I queried, "What happened there?" "Mr Ellis, you were unfortunately thrown in at the deep end. We finance a group of dissidents as part of the attempt to constantly destabilise the East West equilibrium, you don't need to know the detail, but basically what we were trying to do here was put pressure on them, to try and get them to make a mistake. Unfortunately the Russians were totally confused as to what was going on and tried to kill Kurt at the airport to cut off this particular arm of their activities, you see these two are only one cell of a number of people we are watching. The way the Russians work is to have a number of active cells at all times, when one gets into trouble they dispose of it leaving the other intact, none of the cells have any contact with each other and do not know who each other are. Fortunately we had protection in place at

Tegel mainly for you, but it was handy to keep this cell active".

"So what I read in the paper about the Russian rocket at Baikonur failing its test firing makes them even more determined to get our plans" I stated. "Exactly" responded Ralph. My father spoke again, "We know they are after other secret projects and it is highly likely they have other people planted in our department that we don't yet know about". "So where do I come in all this mess? I demanded. "We need you to stay with these guys, and go along with them as far as you can, it is vital that we find out as much from inside their cell as we can" Ralph elaborated. My father continued, "We want you to get as much information as you can about what they know. It's likely they don't know what the projects are that are targeted for theft, but Kurt is possibly a big fish himself, he has diplomatic status and we think he is using it to make it easier to move around. And we suspect he may even be a KGB officer ".

I told them about the briefcase with the compartment, and Ralph said they did not know that was how the diamonds were hidden. Ralph explained they had already had to detain one person in the Ministry as he had worked out they were watching him, this was what I had seen reported in the Daily Telegraph. He also told me that more arrests were imminent. He finished by explaining "What we are asking you to do is very dangerous, your life could be in jeopardy at times. But you have no choice, you will report all you see and hear to Ton, he will be your direct line of contact no-one else. If he becomes unavailable, we will re-contact you, you are under no circumstances to try and contact us here, and we will deny all knowledge of your existence if you do. You are only to have limited contact with your father until this is all over. Do you understand?" "Yes" I replied meekly. Ralph continued "We want you to remain as distant from any contact with us or your father. Because any chance they may have of linking you with our contact will throw the whole thing off course and may put you in immediate danger where we may not be able to protect you" "I understand" I replied. My father added "I have to say I was against getting you involved at first, but you seem to have got yourself in so deep, the only way out now is to help us ". I nodded acceptance of this comment, and knew my father would be quietly seething at my being in any way roped into this whole thing. However at least I knew the truth now and felt more comfortable about it all, at the same time feeling terrified of what was ahead of me.

"Thank you for being here Mr Ellis, unfortunately your father now has to return on the aircraft he came in on early this morning courtesy of the RAF. Doubtless he will be glad to go home and get some sleep as has been working on this for two days now nonstop for your benefit. As I said before, this meeting and conversation never happened as far as we are concerned. Goodbye Mr Ellis". Ralph closed the meeting. Ton escorted me out of the room and to the lift we went down to the basement car park, the driver was waiting for us. I noticed he was carrying a shoulder holster under his unbuttoned jacket. All the way back Ton said nothing to me and we were delivered to his apartment in Amsterdam, on the way up Ton said he would take me home later, he wanted to talk.

"Robert, I am sorry I couldn't explain anything to you last night, as soon as you produced the diamonds I knew I had to refer to higher authority" Ton pleaded. "Ton, you did all the right things, don't feel guilty or sorry about it. You were just going through all the correct procedures" I reassured him. "Well, I'm glad you understand" He replied, looking relieved. "Ton, if there was anyone I would choose to report to in this kind of situation it would be you. I want you to know that it was only you, that I immediately thought of when I got back, to confide in" "Well, I was going to ask you, did you at anytime mention this to anyone else? Diny, or the family you stay with?" he questioned. "No not a soul" I truthfully replied. "Well, that's good" he seemed at ease after this. "We must develop a means of communicating other than face to face or telephone" He said. "Why?" I queried. "Because if they suspect you are having contact with anyone on a regular basis even though we are friends, it will likely put us both in jeopardy, who knows they may already know I'm an agent. No, we must develop a few different places where we can exchange messages."

"What about the normal post?" I questioned, "Yes that's a good secure way to start with, but we need a few even more secure ways. I will arrange for you to have a post office box. And I will also get one for me and you can mail to me when you are away, that will be even more anonymous" he confided. "Ton, something worries me about Kurt and Jaap, I think they are higher up in the hierarchy than Ralph or whoever he really is, thinks, because, on the boat they were both talking about Blue Streak. If they were just a fund raising cell running diamonds they wouldn't need to know that much. I think, they are also going to be the means by which the stolen information gets back as well. Which does reinforce the likelihood that they are both KGB agents" Ton nodded "Good deduction, I will pass that on, they could well be the big fish or at least close to whoever is". "You must take the diamonds back home with you and keep them safe, I don't want them thinking you have got rid of them" Should I put them in a bank deposit box or something?" I asked. "No, they may want you to use them for something, just keep them close to you and don't try to sell them yet." Ton warned.

Chapter 7 - On the right side

I got to work on Monday morning feeling a bit tired after the hectic Sunday's activities, but at least I now had a clearer picture of what I had to do. Jaap met with me in his office and explained that on Wednesday we would go to Hamburg with Kurt and that this would be the last part of the current activity with the diamonds. "There's one thing I don't understand Jaap, those diamonds you gave me, won't they be missed? Won't someone want to know what has happened to them?" I questioned. "We have already told people we had to use them to keep the plan on track and they are OK about it" He tried to explain. "What do I have to do now?" I asked. "You will carry the next shipment in your luggage for us, that way you will have earned the stones you have" He coldly stated. So, I was to become a courier for illegal stones! I better let Ton know about this somehow, I thought to myself. "OK I can do that" I agreed. Jaap seemed pleased about my ease of decision making. "And now the boss wants to see you" he said.

I went to Gerritt's office, which was a small room attached to the residence. He greeted me warmly, "Well done Robert, I'm extremely pleased with the result of your Berlin trip." "Well, it was Jaap and Kurt as well." I stated. "But from what Jaap has told me the idea to solve the impasse was yours and that is what good sales negotiation is about. Now, I've been doing some calculations and the commission from the first years sales should give you around 12,000 guilders in bonus. It will be paid monthly as each order is delivered and paid for. I expect the first payment to come from them in about two weeks, so that should be in your pay at the end of the month. A nice Christmas present huh?" I was staggered, I had no idea the commission was going to be that much! It was almost double what I earned! "Well, I'm very happy of course Gerritt, and I will try to do some more deals in the future." He also explained I was clearly in the lead for the sales competition and that in April when the year's sales were tallied up for each sales person, I would be in the running for the holiday. But he warned that as I had started in November I was actually not that far in front of those sales people that had been going for a full year. The holiday was to be a week for two all expenses paid in Portugal. That seemed a pretty good reward to me!

Gerritt arranged to pick me up from home at 7:00pm that evening to have dinner with him and his wife Elenor. "I understand you like good food?" He queried. "Yes I love good cuisine" I replied. Well, we are going to the Five Flies tonight!" d'Fijff Vlieghen or Five Flies as it's known, is a restaurant in the heart of Amsterdam on Spuistraat, well known for its ambience and good food. The restaurant is made up of several unique and intimate rooms and boasts four original Rembrandt paintings on its walls, Nicolaas Kroese the owner has made it his life's work to achieve international recognition of his restaurant. I was very excited about going there, how many times I had walked past the place as a student two years before promising myself that one day I would be able to afford to eat there.

Gerritt and his wife picked me up at 7:00pm sharp, he drives a Mercedes, nice car! The business must be doing well I thought. We drove into Amsterdam and Gerritt parked the car in a parking station just around the corner from the restaurant. As we walked in, the maitre d'hotel greeted Gerritt as a long lost friend, so he was a regular I thought to myself, not bad. We sat at a window seat and I soaked in the ambience of total luxury, it was a rare experience that I considered I could get used to. The leather bound menu's and wine list were produced and a bottle of KRUG 1953 magically appeared by our side, crystal flutes were filled with the lightly golden liquid, and we toasted our presence at this fount of gastronomic delight. The sharp, pungent, yeasty nose of the champagne teased my palate and as I sipped, the dry yet tingling effect of one of the world's best champagnes made me realise why men and women the world over revere this very special wine.

We studied the menu in virtual silence, and I decided on the pate de foie gras as a starter, I wanted to indulge myself. Gerrit decided on the quail eggs and Elenor chose a chilli prawn dish on a bed of oven roasted peppers. For main course I ordered a tournedo of beef flambe'd with an orange brandy sauce, braised courgettes and small new potatoes glazed with honey and ginger. Gerrit took a stuffed chicken breast filled with mango and avocado with a green salad, Elenor wanted the fillet of plaice grilled and served with a lemon and coriander jus and a greek salad.

All this decision making made us thirsty and we poured another glass of the KRUG. Gerritt asked me how I was settling in to my host family's home, and I explained I had stayed with them before two years ago. I also explained that I had found a female friend in Diny. Gerritt said that I must bring her over to have dinner at their home soon. I accepted the invitation gracefully, I would ask her when she was free I told them.

We spoke of the beauty of the city that is Amsterdam, and how well it had been preserved over the centuries. Gerritt said his father had been on the city council during the war and they had tried desperately to stop the Germans from destroying the city and had mostly succeeded. It had been a long struggle in those times and the toll on his father had been terminal, he died a year after the war ended, saying that his job was done. But Gerritt said many Amsterdammers still bore grudges against the Germans because of what had been done, he was no exception I mused.

The main course was accompanied by a bottle of 1954 Chateau Mouton for Gerritt and myself and a 1957 Pouilly Fuisse for Elenor. The Tournedo was a melt in the mouth piece of beef, and I could understand how this restaurant had achieved such recognition. For desserts we all indulged in chocolate souffle, a speciality of this house. It was heavenly. Finishing with coffee and armagnac for the men and Elenor had a green chartreuse. It was starting to rain as we walked from the restaurant to the car park.

As we drove back to Aalsmeer I was so taken with the style of these two, I told them it was the most elegant evening I had ever had. They thought that was pretty special and were very pleased that I had enjoyed it so much. Whilst the Mercedes sped through the now wet streets of Amsterdam and out past the Olympic Stadium, I turned my thoughts to the week ahead and the Hamburg trip that I would be doing on Wednesday with Kurt and Jaap. "Hamburg is a crazy city Robert" Gerritt seemed to be reading my mind! "How do you mean?" I asked. "Well, during the war it was always a bit on the outer and all the artists and creative people seemed to congregate there, and it hasn't lost its magic since then. You will enjoy it I think. You will be staying at the Atlantic Hotel with Kurt and Jaap, it's very nice there!" This made me very excited about the trip and I forgot temporarily the more sinister side to the visit. The car drew up outside 26 Hadleystraat and I thanked them both once again for a fantastic evening. There were no lights on in the house, so I quietly let myself in and went straight to bed to sleep another night of the kind of blissful sleep one has after having indulged.

On my way to work the next day I thought about what I would do with the bonus I had coming to me. Put it in the bank? Spend it? Or a bit of both? Well I would certainly update my wardrobe I decided, one decent suit and a pair of slacks and a jacket were all I had for business wear, so that would be a priority, maybe I would get Diny to help me choose some new clothes? I mused. I also thought I might take her out to a nice restaurant to celebrate. I would go around and see her tonight before packing for my trip to Hamburg the next day I resolved, I liked being with her and it was a nice escape from all the other stuff going on.

Chapter 8 – It all goes wrong

I went round to Diny's place as soon as I got home after work, the day had been an office day, consisting of studying the files of all the clients in Hamburg and getting an idea of what had to be done there. There had not been many service calls to these customers in the past and it seemed to me there were many opportunities to increase our involvement there. I discussed this with Gerritt and he felt the same way, there had not been anyone really looking after these clients before. I reminded him I still had to go and cover the South of Holland and Belgium yet as well, which really were my proper sales area, but he seemed OK about the excursion into the German market for the moment.

I knocked on the blue painted door of Diny's house and the poodle and her mother came to the door, "She's just gone to the shops, come in and have a coffee, she won't be long" she reassured me. Diny's mother Anja, was around 38 years of age I guessed and a good looking woman, she had passed on her trim, petite, good looks to her daughter. Diny's father Hans, worked in the flower auctions in Aalsmeer as an accountant, he was a cheery and welcoming character, well liked by all who knew him. Hans asked me how work was going as we tucked into coffee and biscuits, I explained I was off to Hamburg in the morning and that I had already earned a nice bonus from the Berlin trip. He seemed pretty impressed and I felt confident he knew I would take care of Diny whenever we went out. Diny appeared at the door of the lounge room and gave me a really lovely smile, looking down as she did, a bit embarrassed to have shown her pleasure at seeing me in front of her parents. We sat and talked about her family's background for a bit. Then Diny suggested we go for a walk. The rain had stopped and although it was still cold, we put our coats on and walked in the opposite direction of the shops. Aalsmeer is situated on the side of a large lake, and to our right the lake glistened with just a hint of ice on the water. The large water tower that dominates the eastern side of the lake was straight in front of us, but tonight was a rare night that did not bring the usual howling winds that accompanies the cold so often in Holland. We talked about Diny's studies at the School of Music, she said she was going to finish the course and then take a year out to travel around Europe. Then she would come back to study more, as she was the same age as me we both agreed we had plenty of time to explore the world as well as make a career. She turned to face me as we reached the roadside by the lake, and said "I have done little else since the dinner at Ton's but think about you and me and how well we get on together, I think it's time we became more than just friends, what do you think?" I was stunned, I had been thinking the same way. "I feel the same way Diny, I think a lot of you and feel very happy when you are with me, I think we should try and see what happens" I looked into her hazel eyes and at her soft brunette hair. I kissed her lips softly and she returned with more pressure, we put our arms around each other and I felt my heart racing. We stood back and smiled at each other, "I think we are going to work out just fine" Diny said confidently. "I hope so because you already mean a lot to me Diny" I replied. "I feel very comfortable with you and I can talk to you about anything, you are intelligent as well as a stunning woman" "Wow! Nobody has called me stunning before" She seemed shocked. "I really think that, and I would be proud if you would let me take you out to dinner when I get back from Hamburg to a really top class restaurant in Amsterdam, your choice!" "Hmm I really love Indonesian food, so I will look forward to that" She said. "Indonesian it is then!" I replied.

We walked further around the side of the lake and then I walked her back home and said goodnight, we parted with another kiss, this time a bit more passionate and I knew this was going to be a special friend I had here. I walked home feeling quite dizzy and disorientated, it was only 8.30 when I got back and Miep my landlady looked puzzled as I walked in, "Where have you been? I had dinner for you and you didn't come back, it's keeping warm in the oven for you" she enquired. "I'm very sorry, I went round to see Diny and didn't mean to be so long, thank you for keeping it warm for me" I apologised. "Oh, so that's where you were, I thought that might have been it, don't worry I can tell by that big grin on your face, you have been up to more important things than dinner!" she stated. "Well we have decided to see a bit more of each other, and she is a lovely person" I tried to play it down a bit. "Diny is a very pretty girl and highly intelligent, and I'm glad to see you both are getting on well together" she confided.

I can't remember eating dinner or packing my bag for Hamburg, I was still reeling from thoughts of Diny. I was smitten I decided, and also resolved to enjoy the moment.

As I was getting into the taxi to Schiphol in the morning, Diny came round the corner to say goodbye, I was so happy to see her, and to once again get a kiss before speeding off to the airport. What a lovely thing to do I thought.

The check in counter was busy and Kurt and Jaap had not arrived when I got there, so I went to the ticket desk and picked up my ticket and checked in and went to the first class lounge to wait for them. They arrived 15 minutes later just in time for the flight to be called, we said brief hello's and walked to the aircraft, it was a Lufthansa Viscount aircraft, the airline had bought a number of these British built aircraft for their fleet to operate short haul flights. It's only a 45 minute flight from Amsterdam to Hamburg so hardly time to have a coffee and biscuit in flight. We arrived at Hamburg airport at 10:15 and took a cab to the Atlantic Hotel. The foyer at the Atlantic is luxurious and plush, and we were checked in with minimal delay and shown to our rooms, having previously agreed to meet in the coffee shop for a sandwich before going out.

Kurt and Jaap had ordered club sandwiches and coffee for us before I got down to meet them, and we tucked in to them with gusto. We discussed what they had to do to deliver the stones that were in my briefcase now sitting at Jaaps feet. I said I would go and do some calls previously arranged with some of our clients. Whilst they went and delivered the stones, and then meet back at the hotel for dinner. They agreed this was a good idea. I really did not want to be there with them, although I would have liked to have eyeballed their contact in Hamburg.

I went off to call on a couple of wholesalers that I had rung on Monday to confirm appointments. They had seemed quite pleased that someone from the company was finally paying them some attention. The first company Von Graaf imports told me that the market for prepacked product was likely to increase greatly in the future as new styles of shops along the lines of the American supermarkets were emerging in Germany. And that with the right pricing they should be able to double the market in twelve months. I showed the new vacuum packs we were producing and they loved the concept, we haggled a bit on prices, but I walked out of there with an order equal to double the entire previous export quantities to all of Germany, with an option to increase further if required. The second company Albert Sigmunder & co was not so fruitful, they were clearly out of touch with their markets and were struggling to stay afloat. The managing director was an old man set in his ways and although happy to see me was doubtful they could do anything with our new technology. It's amazing the difference an attitude makes in running a business. Still, I had a successful day and as my taxi wended its way back from the outer industrial area of Hamburg to the centre of town, my thoughts again turned to Diny and how I would be home tomorrow night, and whether or not I would see her.

I got back to the Hotel at about 5:15 pm and as I walked into the foyer and got my key, the front desk clerk explained there was someone to see me and had been waiting for an hour. I walked over to the gentleman wearing a very smart dark grey suit, and introduced myself "Robert Ellis, I understand you want to talk to me?" "Mr Ellis I am Inspector Rolf Grunholm of Hamburg Special Investigations dept of the directorate of Police in Hamburg, I understand you are staying here with two colleagues Mr Jaap Van den Bosch and Mr Kurt Steiglitz?" He showed his official ID badge. "That is correct Inspector" I confirmed. "Mr Ellis it is with regret that I have to inform you that both your colleagues are dead, killed about two hours ago by an unknown person, shot at point blank range" Do you have any idea what they may have been doing?" "Err, umm, no, I have no idea what their appointment was about or where, I went to cover two calls on clients of the company and they went to do their own calls" I sat down on the couch in the foyer, stunned by the revelation they were dead. "Tell me what you think may have happened Inspector?" I asked. "We have nothing at this time, except that they had an appointment at a warehouse in the north of the city. They must have been surprised by the assassin because there were no signs of a struggle and nothing to suggest they had anything of value to steal if it was just a robbery. Did they have any papers with them or a briefcase?" I thought carefully before answering, "I'm not sure, Jaap did have a briefcase on the plane, as did I, but I'm not sure if they took it with them." It suddenly occurred to me Jaap had my briefcase with him if indeed he had taken it with him, and there was nothing to suggest he wouldn't have, after all that's where the diamonds were.

"Mr Ellis, come with me, I realise you are in great shock about this, but there may be some things you can tell us that may help us to piece some of it together." "Yes of course I replied, I just need to go to my room and get my passport and papers for you if you don't mind?" I asked, "Of course I will wait here" Rolf replied.

I went up in the lift to my room, to my surprise, my briefcase was there! I opened it and checked it was definitely mine, and the stones had been removed, so Jaap must have transferred them to his case then put my case back in my room. I lifted the phone, and rang Ton's number in Amsterdam. He answered. "Ton, listen to me I haven't got much time, but it's all gone wrong here, they are both dead and I'm being taken in by the police to make a statement, I don't know if they know what's going on but they aren't giving anything away if they do." Ton asked which station I was going to and I told him I didn't know, but gave him the name of the Inspector. "Leave it with me I'll have you out of Hamburg tonight, but in the meantime co-operate with them but don't tell them anything, do you understand?" "Yes, yes of course Ton, thanks." I hung up and rushed to the lift with my briefcase in hand, to meet the Inspector, we walked out of the foyer into his waiting car, and went to Hamburg West Police station. I was questioned and asked to account for everything that had happened from the moment we boarded the Lufthansa flight that morning, I told them about my calls and gave them the names of the people I had seen, of course omitting the conversation with Jaap and Kurt at lunchtime. After about three hours of questioning Inspector Rolf came in and explained there was someone from the British Consulate in Hamburg to see me, he was a little perplexed as to how they had found out I was helping them, but seemed OK about it. The man from the consulate asked for the policemen to leave us alone in the room, and they left, he looked around the room for any signs of recording devices. Then he sat facing me. "Mr Ellis, my name is Peter Whittington, you are in great danger, I have to get you out of here and back to Amsterdam, right now." "And how are we going to do that?" I questioned rather curtly. "My people are organising a seat on a flight for you right now, a KLM flight at 19:30hrs, your luggage is being picked up from the Atlantic Hotel now. We are also explaining to the authorities here that you are senior government personnel working under cover for us here. They will understand this and release you immediately." "Sounds a bit farfetched to me" I replied. "Mr Ellis, I am under orders to get you out of here and your attitude of indifference is not helping me to protect you!" He almost yelled at me. "I'm sorry, I suppose I'm shocked by all that has happened, and I don't mean to be ungrateful for your prompt actions" I apologised. "That's OK it's understandable in the circumstances, you did the right thing to alert Ton to what had happened, we knew there had been a shooting but not who had been shot."

The Inspector knocked on the door and Peter invited him in, "Mr Ellis, Mr Whittington, you are free to go, my superiors are satisfied with your statement and now understand fully the gravity of your situation. I have a car waiting to take you to the airport, the flight leaves in half an hour. We will have to take you straight to the plane. We both got into the car and Peter sat next to me in the back. The Inspector sat next to the driver, the Inspector had his police revolver in his hand and kept looking around to the back and sides of the car as we sped out to the airport with sirens and lights. We arrived at the airport only 16minutes after leaving the hotel and went straight through the barrier to the airside part of the terminal and the car drew up by the front stairs of the KLM Electra. Inspector Grunholm turned and said "Mr Ellis, If we ever meet again I hope it's under better circumstances, have a safe flight!" I almost expected him to click his heels as he stood and said this!

I almost ran to the stairs, Peter had handed me a boarding pass, handed to him by one of the ground staff when we drew up at the aircraft's side. I settled into the now familiar leather upholstery of KLM First Class, and was pleased with the anonymity provided by the aircraft. All I wanted to do now was get home.

The flight to Amsterdam was quick and uneventful, I got through immigration and claimed my bags and went through customs. I had bought a bottle of Cognac for Ton and some perfume for Diny on board the flight. Now all I wanted was to go home and see Diny. She was beginning to mean a lot to me I thought. Maybe I was reading too much into the relationship. As I came out of customs the familiar voice of Ton greeted me from behind, "This way I have car waiting" I handed him the cognac I had bought for him as he whisked me out to a waiting Bentley with the engine running. I got into the back seat and Ton sat next to the driver. "Well, we lost that cell Mr Ellis!" The voice of Ralph boomed at me from the other rear seat. "Sorry to have you torn away so suddenly old chap, but you were in some danger, the other side obviously cottoned on to the fact we were watching them, and disposed of their own to protect the rest" "You mean they killed their own people? " I demanded. "Oh yes, old boy, no respect amongst these chaps you know, they just take what they want and throw it away when it is of no further use." "So what happens now?" I asked. Well we need to do a debrief right now with you, then you go home and wait for them to recontact you" He seemed so matter of fact about it all, it irritated me. "They will want to contact me, why?" I asked. "Well, you have information about their now extinct agents and the stones." "No the stones were with Jaap" I explained. "Yes but you still have the other stones that he gave you and they will likely want them back now" Ralph dryly said. I thought of the half a million guilders worth of diamonds sitting in a box under my bed at Hadleystraat. What on earth was going to happen?

I was about to explain to Ralph that I really didn't want to go on with this anymore, and go back to my normal boring uneventful life, but the car turned into an underground parking lot somewhere in Amsterdam West, one of the new buildings. We got out and entered a lift. The lift stopped at the fifth floor, and Ralph and Ton took me to a room, it had no windows and was bereft of furniture save a desk and three chairs. Ralph sat behind the desk and pulled a tape recorder out of the drawer, turned it on and said "Now Mr Ellis, tell me all that has happened since 08:00hrs this morning."

I went through everything that had transpired, referring to my notes occasionally, the meeting at lunchtime and that they had obviously arranged to meet someone to hand over the last of the stones. "You don't think they just killed them because they had delivered do you?" I asked Ralph. "Maybe, but unlikely, we are trying to get more details from the German police at this time to try and piece together what happened. No, Mr Ellis, we think there is much more to this than meets the eye, we think these guys were much bigger fish, you told Ton you suspected that didn't you?" "Yes I did, but why have them killed?" "Things are not all that they seem in our murky world Mr Ellis. You have been of great help and you have had a big day. Once again this meeting never happened, and the driver will take you home in a less conspicuous vehicle. Ton will keep you posted as to any developments; meantime go about your life in a normal way"

Normal, normal!! He had said, what's normal? I pondered, as the driver bounced along in the less than comfortable Volkswagen on the way home. One thing that was normal was getting home and seeing the pot plants in the window. I thanked the driver and walked up the tiny path to the front door. Miep opened it, "You are a day early young man! What happened?" "Oh, I got all the calls done and doubled our sales in Germany, so caught an earlier flight, just to get back in time to have dinner with you" I chirped cheekily. "Well, there's a thing! What do you know Diny? the boyfriend is back!" I went into the sitting room and there was Diny! Oh, I was so pleased to see her. I gave her a big hug and a kiss and almost forgot Miep was looking on. "Steady on you two! He's only been away a day!" Diny explained she had come round to see Guda, Miep's daughter but she was out, so she was just about to leave when I arrived. "How would you like to come to Portugal with me around Easter time Diny?" "What!" She exclaimed, "Well with the extra business I have secured in Hamburg it just about guarantees me the holiday for two!" "I'm not sure if my parents would let me go with you, they might think you were whisking me away to take advantage of me?" She pleaded. "If I wanted to do that I could do it a lot closer to home!" I blurted out, blushing, I realised I had let my imagination carry me away. "Sorry Diny, that was a bit uncalled for" I apologised. "Don't worry I was quite flattered that you might want to whisk me away!" She smiled with a naughty look on her face like a child that had been caught out stealing a cake.

I walked her home with my arm around her, and didn't want to even think about explaining of the horrors I had experienced today, it all seemed a world away while I was with her. "How would you like to go to Groningen at the weekend with me?" She asked. "I've never been there before, that would be fun" I replied. Well, my aunt and uncle are going to Switzerland on Friday and they come back on Monday. They are going skiing there, and they often ask me to mind their place for them. So we could have some time together there in peace and quiet. "Would your parents mind, you know, the both of us?" I questioned. "Dear, I'm 18, like you an adult almost, they trust me and I know they trust you" "They do?" I asked. "Yes. My dad likes you and Mum thinks you are great too, they are happy for me" "You don't think this is all moving too quickly do you Diny?" "Absolutely not!" She retorted. "We'll take the train to Groningen and have a great weekend" I walked back looking forward to the day after tomorrow when we would take the evening train to go away for the weekend, I decided I would give her the perfume I had bought on the way.

I was dreading going to work, but I got there early as usual. Gerritt said hello and asked why I was home early I told him about the new orders and he was ecstatic. He didn't seem to know about Jaap and Kurt so I thought it best to leave it until he found out. The rest of the day was spent doing the paperwork for the extra orders and planning my trip the following week to Belgium. I thought it best to just carry on as Ralph had suggested as if nothing had happened.

I spent Friday checking out some orders for Berlin that were ready to be shipped and rang Berlin to let them know we were dispatching, they were pleased we were on schedule. I couldn't wait to get home and pack and jump on the train to Groningen with Diny, it would be pure escape!

Chapter 9 – Weekend away

I didn't hang around for the usual Friday after work drinks at the packing shed. I just wanted to escape from the crazy world I had allowed to descend on me, and be with Diny.

I got home as fast as I could pedal my bike, and packed my small suitcase, just as I had finished, the door bell rang and there was Diny with a backpack and a big smile. I gave her a peck on the cheek, told Miep where we were going and tore off down to the bus station with Diny. "What's the rush? The train doesn't go till 6:30!" she questioned. "I just want to get there in plenty of time, I hate being late" I pleaded. We bounced along in the bus along the narrow streets to Centraal Station, and bought tickets, we had about 20mins before the train left, so got on board to secure nice seats for ourselves. It was very cold and windy and as it was only a few weeks until Christmas, the station was busy with people catching trains going home for the weekend and those arriving to do their shopping.

We sat together and I held Diny's hand, "How long does the trip take to Groningen?" I asked. "Oh, we'll be there by 8:00pm, and Aunt Gerda has left plenty of food for us, she rang me this afternoon to tell us to have a good time and enjoy the wine she has left for us" "Oh how nice of her" I said. "Tell me about the house there?" "Well, it's not far from the station, we can walk, and it's a typical old Dutch house with a small garden and 2 stories, with 2 bedrooms and a big kitchen, and dining area, with a cosy front room looking out over a park. It's very nice and it will give us some time together" I thought out loud "I like being with you Diny it's like two friends who have known each other for years, it's very comfortable" "Well I feel like that too!" she confirmed. We snuggled closer together on the seats and sat quietly as the train pulled out of the station, like most rail systems the departure out of Amsterdam is not picturesque, running past the dock area, and then the suburbs. Eventually out into the flat Dutch countryside broken up only by the occasional canal and windmill amongst the polders. At night there's not much to see apart from the odd lighted house here and there. Diny fell asleep on my shoulder, and I dozed off too, glad of the quiet time and to have a good stare at her pretty face without her knowing, the smile on her lips that I longed to kiss. Diny did not wear much makeup and I liked that, her skin was fair but very fine, her figure was petite and well proportioned, and I gazed at her pretty eyes now shut and resting.

About 15 minutes before we got to Groningen she woke and breathed deeply and stretched. I was still staring at her and she was suddenly aware I had been watching her, she blushed and said "having a good look huh?" "I like what I see" I confirmed. "Well, I'm pleased about that, because I can't change much!" "Don't ever change anything, it's all perfect as far as I'm concerned"

The train pulled into the station and we walked off the platform to the ticket barrier, showed our tickets and turned left outside. The house was literally 5 minutes walk away. A very pretty frontage, with red and white shutters around the outside of the windows. Diny took a key from her bag, and let us in the front door, the smell of well polished wooden floors greeted us, there were rugs in the hallway that were obviously old and antique, the whole house gave a feeling of warmth and love.
"What a beautiful house!" I exclaimed. "It is lovely" She confirmed. "Now let's leave our bags here and get some food I'm starving" she said. "Good idea" I agreed. "But first, come here" She demanded, she grabbed my arm and put it around her waist, and pressed her lips to mine, she opened her mouth and our first really passionate kiss took place. I could smell her wonderful body next to mine, and I felt my heart race, I was experiencing feelings I had never had before. "Wow!" I exclaimed. "That was something special" "Get used to it Robert, I have feelings for you I've never had before, and I'm not going to hold back any more" She stated firmly. "Oh I nearly forgot I have a present for you my little Diny" I went to my bag and pulled out the perfume and gave her the gift wrapped package, she eagerly unwrapped it. "Nina Ricci! Oh wow I love that! Thank you my darling" she exclaimed "How did you know?" she queried. "I didn't I just thought it would suit you, it's an elegant perfume, for an elegant lady" she smiled and gave me another passionate kiss. She turned and went to the kitchen. I followed and she pulled out a bottle of Bordeaux from her aunt's collection. "Let's have a drink and make some dinner and enjoy being just us" she

stated. We drank the wine and cooked some veal in a white sauce, with cauliflower and beans and potatoes. It was delicious. There were some cheeses, so we finished off the red wine with that.

We sat on the couch, and cuddled and talked about her week at university, she had an exam coming up, and was quite nervous about it. She had to play some Chopin to an audience of examiners. But she said she knew the music well, it was just the first time she had played to a critical audience, and that was scary. Her aunt had a piano in the front room and she sat and played a part of the piece she was to be examined on. It was beautiful and she played it well. I applauded as she finished and she got up and made a bow to her singular audience. "That was beautiful my love" I said. I went to her and embraced her and we kissed again, this time with even more intent. "I'm ready for bed, it's been a big day" she said. "Me too" I replied. "I'll take the back room, you can have the bigger bedroom" I said. "No darling" She interjected, "we only need one room" "What!" I exclaimed. "I want to share my bed with you tonight" she stated very firmly. "I err, umm, I'm really not sure that's a good thing to do so early in our relationship" I stammered "Just shut up and come here" She demanded. "I know what I want" she was quite fiery about it. "Well, I have to tell you I've err, never done this before to be perfectly honest" "Neither have I" she said. "But I want you tonight!" We took our bags up to the front bedroom and I was very nervous and at the same time really excited and aroused that this young woman wanted me so much. She walked up to me and said "Undress me please" I was all fingers and thumbs and my heart was racing at a million miles an hour. I kissed her in the hope it would relax me, I undid her blouse, and cupped her left breast in my hand and with my other hand tried to undo the back of her bra, but I had no idea what I was doing. She laughed "I can see I'm going to have to give you lessons in this, you really are a virgin" I laughed with her and said, "The lessons will be very enjoyable I'm sure." She turned her back to me so I could see what I was doing, and I managed to get the hooks undone, she turned to face me and her bra fell to the floor. I cupped her soft breasts in my hands and she shivered in excitement, I kissed her neck and then her right breast, as I did this she undid my shirt and then my belt. We kissed passionately again, and I undid her skirt, we both now got rid of the rest of our clothes and slid under the fresh clean sheets. We spent an hour or more just exploring each other's bodies, hardly saying a word. Then she said softly "make love to me now" I was very nervous and I did not want to spoil the magic, but I asked "I have never done this before, so I will try and be very gentle" She smiled and pulled me over on top of her. "I have never done this before either, and it may not be perfect the first time, but I want you so much" I was completely aroused by now and as I pushed into her, I felt her flinch and she let out a small cry. "Is it OK?" I asked, she paused and looked up at me, "yes my love, I'm fine, I'm just no longer a virgin!" and she giggled. We made slow and very passionate love and I felt myself close to orgasm, when she let out a scream "Oh now my love! Come with me!" I felt her contractions as she spasmed in ecstasy, and I came at the same time.

After a few minutes of laying together in each other arms completely spent, we gathered enough breath and energy to kiss again. "That was amazing" I said, "I feel all light and dizzy and wonderfully happy" She looked over at me and said "I think I'm going to become a sex maniac now with you!" We lay there for half an hour just cuddling. And then we fell asleep for what must have been a couple of hours, I woke to find her exploring me again, and she whispered "I want you again my love".

We made love 5 times that night, and woke up at 10:00am, I went down and made coffee and brought it back up to the bedroom. We got showered and dressed without saying much to each other. We went down to the kitchen for breakfast. "This has been the best day in my life so far" she stated in a very definite way. "I just don't want it to stop" I agreed with her.

It was Saturday and we went out to explore the city and do some shopping, Groningen is Holland's seventh largest city and a diverse cultural centre for North Holland, it has its own university and is very proud of the well preserved churches and old buildings going back many centuries. It also boasts many cafés and restaurants, so we shopped for dinner that evening as we had decided to have dinner at home. But we stopped at a little café with one of those typical Dutch terrasses, glassed in frontages of cafes where you can sit and enjoy the winter sun without the cold and wind, as they are heated. We ate lunch as if we had never seen food before. And we both whispered "it must be the sex!" and laughed. We walked back to the house and it was already 3:30pm and starting to get dark. As we got indoors, the phone rang, it was Diny's mother checking that we were OK and Diny told her everything was fine and we would be back on Sunday evening around 6pm. As she put the phone down, she looked into my eyes and said "This is it isn't it?" "What is?" I responded. "You and me, I mean it's perfect the relationship" "Diny I hate to be a pessimist. But we've only known each other a few weeks and yes I agree it's wonderful I've never felt like this before about anything or anyone, and I fell for you the moment I saw you. I think we need to give ourselves more time though. I really do want it to work out. I think I err, I mean I feel like I'm in love with you" she smiled as I clumsily said this, "And I feel that way too my love, come to bed with me again and let me check you haven't fallen out of love with me yet. Let's see if we can improve our techniques, after all practice makes perfect!" With that she took my hand and led me upstairs, we undressed and made love in a much more spontaneous and relaxed way than before. It was heaven, all thoughts of the horrors of the previous week were completely out of my mind.

Diny and I woke from our lovemaking around 7:30pm. We went downstairs and had a glass of white wine, before cooking a hearty dinner of chicken breasts poached in the rest of the white wine, with herbs we had bought, and sprouts, carrots and boiled potatoes. The sprouts had grated nutmeg over them as is often the way they are served in Holland. We washed it all down with a bottle of excellent Burgundy. After coffee we decided to listen to some records Diny's aunt had, some jazz and some classical. But after about an hour and it was still only 10:30 the lure of more carnal pleasures beckoned us both back to bed. We were insatiable.

On the Sunday morning we woke at 11:00am sated from the many sexual forays of the night. We were locked in each other's arms and I looked into her eyes, she was far away. "What are you thinking?" I questioned. "I was wondering how we will both remember this weekend when we are old and grey" "Well, I will certainly have a smile on my face whenever I do" I replied cheekily. "Robert, I hope this is the start of a life together for you and I" she said very candidly. "Well, you know I've been thinking that sort of thing myself" I replied. "I mean we have to give it time, but right now that's all I really want" She started to cry, "What on earth is wrong?" I was very confused. "Nothing, it's just that I'm so happy" tears welled in my eyes too and we both hugged each other until we stabilised our thoughts. It is then that I realised love is a terribly fragile thing and you have to grab every moment for what it is and let nothing get in your way. I told Diny these thoughts, and she said it was a beautiful thing to say, and we better remember that when we encountered difficult times. How prophetic that was to be.

We spent the rest of the day, having a sort of brunch and tidying the house. "We better wash the bedding she said, it stinks of sex!" "Your aunt will know anyway" I said. "How?" she queried. "Come on don't tell me she doesn't suspect we came here for just that?" "Well, she did ask me lots of questions about you, and I did tell her I really thought you were special" "Well, you're right we still need to wash the bedding, but not before I have you once more!" I demanded. "Oh now we are getting frisky aren't we? You weren't as forward as that yesterday. It's about time you started to tell me what you really think and forget your inhibitions." I grabbed her and pushed her back on to the bed, we both had no time for undressing we just proceeded to have what can only be described as full on sex. "Now that was lust!" She exclaimed. "Yes and I think for the first time I really let go of my inhibitions" I said firmly "Well, it was great!" she said. Now I want you to do it very slowly and gently, we still have three hours before the train goes. We got back into bed and this time she took the lead doing things to tease me that I'd never imagined before. "Where did you learn all this?" I asked. "I have read a lot of books on sexual techniques, and my mother and I have a very open relationship, she and dad still have great sex and she has told me a lot of things that she thought I ought to know." "Does she know we might be doing this here?" I asked. "She told me to be honest with my feelings and allow them to direct my actions" "I don't know how I'm going to face her when she realises" I said, "She won't ask stupid questions and she trusts you" she calmed me.

We put the washing on about an hour before we had to go and hung it out just prior to leaving. We walked to the station and the train was on time, we just sat and held each other all the way back to Amsterdam. Then got the bus back to Aalsmeer, I walked her home, and her dad invited me in for coffee. I was terrified they would not approve of our excursion. But instead her mother was extremely welcoming and asked if we had enjoyed our weekend away, my blush must have given the whole thing away, because she completely changed the subject after that. I left for Hadleystraat after half an hour and told Diny I would come round Monday evening, her mother asked me to have dinner with them and I accepted graciously, any excuse to have more time in Diny's company was good by me.

I arrived home to be greeted by Miep, she had coffee ready and was eager to hear about my weekend away. "How did it go?" she asked. "It was wonderful, Diny and I are madly in love" I wanted to say. But my usual shyness prevented me from saying that. "It was great, we spent a lot of time talking and getting to know each other better" I said. "Did you sleep together?' She asked very bluntly. "Miep, I'm not sure if you are joking?" "No, I'm asking a straight question, did you make love, because you two are made for each other, if you didn't, then maybe you need some advice!" "Miep!, we slept together OK?, it was wonderful, we were both virgins and now we are lovers and very much in love, we had a great time! But that's for your ears and nobody else's OK?" "Well I think that's great!" she retorted. "I'm sorry, Miep, to be yelling at you, but I feel very personal about these things, and I know you think like you are my own mother, but there are just some things a son doesn't even share with his mother or anybody else. But I do think I love Diny and she is the best thing that I have right now. Now if you will excuse me I'm going to bed." I stomped off upstairs to my room feeling like I had been cross questioned by the Gestapo. But I know Miep did not mean to pry, she was just trying to protect me from being hurt.

I fell into a troubled sleep knowing that I had to get back to reality in the morning and probably tell Diny what was really going on.

Chapter 10 – A strange turn of events

When I got to work in the morning Gerritt met me and explained that Jaap was sick and wouldn't be in for the week. And would I like to just do his work in the office for the week, it would help me to familiarise with the ordering system and how it meshed in with packing of orders. "Sick! I asked are you sure?" "Yes, his family rang to say he had been taken ill" I didn't labour the point as I wasn't sure if Gerritt was in on the whole scheme of theirs, but it certainly seemed strange. Once in the office, I rang Ton to tell him, and he was surprised but not alarmed. He explained that the Hamburg police still had not confirmed the identity of the dead people, so he would have to wait for positive ID from them. I told him I wanted to see him as soon as possible, but he said it would have to wait till Tuesday as he was out tonight.

I sat in the office and could not understand what the heck was going on, but resolved not to let it get to me. I was still looking forward to having dinner with Diny and her parents. I decided to take a plant for Anja and a good bottle of red for us all to enjoy. Then I got on with the office work. I was actually pleased to have a week at home instead of travelling because it meant Diny and I could spend more time together. The day was pretty routine and I walked out at 5:30, and headed home as fast as I could. As I got in, Miep was busy doing her housework. I asked her "Miep? You don't think I'm becoming too obsessed with Diny too soon do you?" "Robert, you can only follow your heart in these things, you are obviously head over heels in love with her and I'm glad to see you both so happy." It was a diplomatic reply, but I sensed she thought it was typical young love, and decided whatever she said it wouldn't make any difference to my behavior, and she was probably right.

I had bought a large Anthurium plant in full flower on the way home and a bottle of Nuits St George. My bonus was in the bank, so the expense didn't really worry me.

And with Christmas in a few weeks it was good I had the bonus, because I needed to go shopping! I scurried around to Diny's place and arrived on the dot of 7pm as agreed. "Right on time, as I expected" Diny greeted me. Anja was very impressed with the plant and Hans inspected the wine with relish saying it was a great choice to go with the lamb we were going to eat.

I went to help Anja in the kitchen as she had accepted my offer to help chop the vegetables. "Robert, you have no idea how happy Diny is with you" she stated as we prepared the food. "Well I'm very happy with the situation too, I have a great deal of feeling for her." "I know all about the weekend, Diny and I have no secrets, she has had a few boyfriends over the past few years, but has never felt like this about any of them." I responded "She told me how close you are and I think that's fabulous that you talk so openly, I hope I can be that honest with you and Hans too?" I asked "Of course, there are no secrets in this house." "Well I want you to know, that I will do my very best to look after Diny whenever she is with me, and respect her as a very best friend above all else."

Anja looked at me with a very direct eye contact "Robert, Diny means the world to me and Hans. We are overjoyed you seem to have unlocked a new happiness in her, I know you are lovers now, and that she wanted to give herself to you in the most intimate way any woman can. But please understand from a mother's point of view, she is still my child and nothing will ever come to surpass the love a mother has for her offspring. I want you to know that Hans and I like you very much and hope that you and Diny will work hard to make this relationship work." "Wow!" I exclaimed. "That is a big statement, but I will try, and I know Diny will too, to always respect the love you both have for her and to behave as responsible adults. I think you are a very special woman too and Hans is a very fortunate man to have two beautiful and mature woman in his life" She blushed as I said she was a special woman, but I really meant what I said, and she knew it. "Robert, you and I will get along just fine if you keep that attitude, I like the way you respect females, it's unusual for one so young as you. Now let's go and join the other two before I fall in love with you as well" I now blushed at what she said, and it must have shown as we walked in to the front room, because Diny looked up and gave a querying look. I looked away but could see she was intrigued. She made an excuse to talk to her mother and they disappeared into the kitchen. A few minutes later they came back and we all sat and talked about the coming Christmas time. They wanted me to come round and share Christmas day with them, and I couldn't think of a better place to be, so accepted graciously.

Diny asked me to come out and help her get the plates on to the table, so I followed her and she shut the door to the kitchen, stood with her hands on her hips and glared at me "I'd better watch my step with you Romeo! Now I find you are trying to seduce my mother!" "What! What on earth are you talking about' I stammered. She laughed, "You silly boy, now you have two women in this house madly in love with you, my mother thinks you are just the best and told me not to lose you under any circumstances, so my father better watch out!" "Oh my god, Diny I didn't mean to create that kind of impression, I mean, I err, well I don't know anymore" Don't worry we were just joking, but she does think you are great, she asked me what the lovemaking was like as well" "Oh heck, what did you say" I pleaded "I told her whilst I didn't have anything to compare you with in other men, but I got wet just thinking about it now, and she cut me off at that point saying that was enough detail to know it was just perfect!" "I've never been in a family that shares so much, it's difficult for me to understand" I bemoaned. "Don't worry darling, it's just that you should be proud that both my parents like you so much and accept you, now let's go and eat I'm starving"

I ate dinner with the thoughts in my mind that these parents knew I had bedded their daughter, no, correction, she bedded me come to think of it! Who anyway, was a virgin but no longer, and they still liked me, I always thought parents chased young men down the street with shotguns when they found out they had deflowered their daughter. This family was quite enjoying it.

The dinner was great, Hans got a little drunk having opened a bottle of cognac after dinner and whilst I had one glass, he had several. Anja was relaxed and happy and the whole evening was a success. Diny insisted on walking me home, and we walked out into the cold night air, hugged together against the wind. She kissed me as we walked out the door and on the way, told me she wanted to see me tomorrow night, I explained I had to go and see Ton, but Wednesday night we could go out and have a meal, so she settled on that. I fell into bed in a somewhat euphoric state, and had no trouble sleeping.

The next day at work nothing was said about Jaap, and the whole day was a blur of paperwork and order queries. I looked at my watch and it was 5:15pm, I rushed out of the place, straight to the station to catch a bus to Beethovenstraat and Ton's place, he had already asked me to eat with him, Jaanus was away so it would be just him and me. Ton's cheery face welcomed me at the door, and he immediately poured a glass of Jenever for us both. We sat and Ton said, "Robert, I'm not sure if Jaap and Kurt really are dead! I mean there's been no positive ID and it should have been easy. It may be it's just a cover to hide them for a while." I asked "Ton those diamonds I have are really worrying me, they are not in a secure place, and I feel like I have stolen goods in my care." Ton replied "You realise that as far as the authorities are concerned if they are not claimed or identified within three months of you having told us about them, they are yours officially, they are classified as salvage, and I can then sell them for you legally" "What!" I exclaimed, "There's half a million guilders worth there!" "Actually probably more like Dfl 650,000 in my opinion there's some nice stones there, I had a good look at them when you left them with me" Ton explained. "That would buy you and Diny a very nice house" He smiled as he said it. "Yes it would, and by the way while we are talking about Diny, I have my first bonus and I want to blow some of it on a ring for Diny for Christmas, what do you suggest?" I was glad to change the subject. "Well how much do you want to spend?" He asked. "Anything up to 6,000 guilders, that's half my bonus" I said. "Wow, I could do you a good ring for that, at wholesale of course" He assured me. "Now let's have a look what I have here" He went and retrieved a large locked steel box from his safe. Now it's not going to be an engagement ring is it?" He queried.

"Heck no, we haven't got that far yet" I explained. "OK, so it's a sort of friendship thing right?" I nodded. "Well, if I set a nice diamond in the centre of a cluster of amethyst's that would look good. There's a lovely blue white here about 40 points, then six 10 point amethysts around it would look spectacular, set in a beveled setting of white gold. You'll have change out of 4,000 guilders, so you can take her out for a good dinner and maybe even an overnight at the Kras with the rest?" The "Kras" was local terminology for "The Krasnapolsky Hotel" A 5 star hotel on the Damrak itself, just the best place to stay in Amsterdam.

"Sounds good to me Ton, I confirmed, can you do it by Christmas?" "I can have it ready by Thursday if you want, but let's say Friday evening you can pick it up." "Great" I confirmed. "That's why you really wanted to talk to me was it?" "Yes it was Ton, I love this girl and I want to give her the best" Ton looked at me and warned, "Don't breath a word about all the other stuff to her, or anyone, understand?" "Yes of course Ton" I agreed. "Good, now let's eat, I've got some good steak here and bottle of Lafite to celebrate your new love. You are lovers, right?" "Oh Ton, why does everybody want to know if we have slept together?" 'Because it's what lovers do! You silly boy" He chided. "Now let's enjoy!" We celebrated as good friends and Ton brought out the stones while we sampled the Lafite, and I held them in my hand trying to picture them on Diny's finger. "Ton, I have no idea what size her finger is!" I exclaimed. "Don't worry it was one of the first things I looked at when you brought her here, I know exactly" He comforted. "You old rascal Ton, I'll bet you look at all women's fingers first?" "Oh not always the fingers first, especially good looking young girls like Diny, but second!" He laughed.

It was a great night, I nearly missed the last bus home due to Ton's insistence we have multiple Armagnac's after dinner. So it was well after midnight when I finally fell into a somewhat alcoholic slumber.

Chapter 11 – Christmas shopping and a shock

Diny and I went out to the local café on the Wednesday evening, a few glasses of wine and some chicken risotto, it was nice and relaxed. "I need to do some Christmas shopping Diny, will you help me?" "Of course my love, I need to do some too it's the end of next week you know?' she reminded me. "Yes, it is, let's go to Amsterdam on Saturday all day" "Good idea" she agreed. "Then I get you all to myself for a whole day" I smiled. "Something even better, Anje and Hans are going out to Hans's Christmas function on Saturday night and staying in Rotterdam, they asked me if I wanted you to stay, and I said yes" She revealed. "Oh, are you sure it's OK?" I was still nervous about her parents and the fact they would know we would obviously sleep together in their house. "If you are worried about making love to me in my own home then you can sleep on the couch!" She chided. "I think I will cast my worries aside on that one" I said boldly. She laughed "I thought you would" We walked to her home and it was only 9: 00pm, but I told her I needed an early night, saw her to her door and wandered back to Hadleystraat.

The next day Thursday, was as uneventful as any work day could be. But Gerritt came by and told me that it was unlikely anyone would beat me at the sales target and he was pretty sure it would be mine, so would I like him to make the booking, and who would be accompanying me. I told him Diny would be my partner. He told me we would be staying at a place on the Portuguese Algarve coast called Monte Gordo, the hotel was right on the beach, and we would have 7 days paid accommodation and meals, airfares, transfers, and 3 day car hire, plus $1,000 US for spending money. He would make the booking for the week after Easter. "It will be quiet then," he said. I told him it was a most generous prize. And he said "Robert, since you joined our company you have brought many millions of guilders in new business to our company, it needs to be rewarded. The other sales people will receive their bonuses too in keeping with their efforts" He also said that initially he had reservations about employing a foreigner, but because I spoke such fluent Dutch and had a good attitude he gave me a chance. It was great to have such a positive report from my boss, for whom I'd only worked for six weeks!

I couldn't wait to tell Diny we were definitely going to Portugal, but I thought I'd make it part of her Christmas present, although she already knew I was in contention. I went home feeling really good. But when I got home, there was a message from Ton to ring him urgently, I went down the street to the phone box and rang his number. "Robert, I have confirmation that the two bodies were not Jaap and Kurt, from the police in Hamburg, so it's obviously a ruse to hide them for while. The good news is we have done a sweep of passenger lists on all flights out of Germany since last Friday and their names do not appear. I would say they are back in Russia or are holed up somewhere in Germany for the time being." I thanked him for the info and asked if there was anything I should do, he said no just keep your eyes open and act normally, and to be at his place to pick up the ring tomorrow night. "Oh yes of course" I told him. "I will bring the money"

I got an early night and didn't even talk to Diny that evening, she said she had some studying to do, and I was happy to actually sit and watch TV for few hours before getting an early night. The next morning Friday, I went to work and just flowed through the day as if I had done this all before, went to the bank to withdraw the money, and got out of the place on the crack of 5pm. I jumped on the 5:35pm bus to Beethovenstraat, eager to see the ring Ton had made. I rang the bell and he let me in. "Robert, this is possibly the loveliest ring I have ever made!" He was jubilant. As a master silversmith and goldsmith as well as a revered diamond merchant it had to be something special for him to crow about. The ring sat in a velvet lined black box on his table, and it sparkled like nothing else I had ever seen! "Oh Ton! It's stunning" I exclaimed. "I have set it on a base of white gold with a cavity in the bottom so that the light will shine through the diamond and show the beauty of all the 40 points! There are no feathers in the stone, it is as close to perfect as you could get. The amethysts are set with a beveled edge so it won't catch on anything, and the way they are set will also catch as much light as possible. Although I have cut and set much bigger stones in my time, this is just wonderful" He was so proud, and it was truly magnificent. "Ton it is just sensational, and I thank you with all my heart!" I was close to tears, the ring just sat there, the fire and colour coming from the diamond was just amazing. I wondered what Diny would say on Christmas morning when I gave it to her, and how her mother and father would react. That excitement was still to come! I paid Ton the cash it came to 3,800dfl and Ton said retail it would have fetched around 8,000Dfl, so I was very pleased! I put the ring in my briefcase and locked it. Ton asked me to stay but I figured I should spend at least one evening at home. I jumped on the bus and got back around 7:30pm, just in time for dinner, Miep was pleased I was having an evening at home. "Diny came round to see if you were about earlier, but I told her you were out, and she said she would come round about 9:30 in the morning to go shopping with you" I thanked Miep for passing on the message. "Miep I will be staying at Diny's place tomorrow night just so you know" "Yes, she told me, she was very excited and wanted one of my recipe's so you will have a great meal with what she has planned. But you're probably more interested in the after meal activities I would guess?" "Oh Miep, you are a tease!" I chided her. "Miep how well can you keep a secret?" I was dying to show her the ring. "Well, I kept a few during the war" she muttered. I took the ring out of my briefcase and handed her the box. "This is Diny's Christmas present I picked up tonight" She opened it so carefully as if she suspected some joke snake would leap out at her. "Oh my goodness, it's the most beautiful thing I've ever seen in my life, she will have a heart seizure when she sees this Robert" "I hope not quite as dramatic as that Miep! But I think she will like it" The ring then became the topic of conversation over dinner and I made them all promise to keep the secret, I was sure they would.

Diny was there early Saturday morning to meet me and she was already sipping coffee with Miep when I came down. "Hello stranger, haven't seen you for 1 and half days, I was getting withdrawal symptoms" She smiled as she said it, her lips curling up in her cheeky grin. I gave her a peck on the cheek, and sat down beside her, Miep poured me a coffee and I buttered an egg biscuit and coated it with chocolate hail so beloved by the Dutch. I went upstairs and cleaned my teeth and grabbed my money, and we walked to the bus stop. "I'd really like to get something nice for both Anje and Hans for Christmas, and also Miep and the family" I explained on the bus to Centraal Station. "What about me?" She complained. "Oh I nearly forgot you!" I joked. "Don't worry darling, I have some very special things for you" I reassured her. She tried to question me "Tell me, Tell me, It's not fair I have to wait a week to know" she pleaded, Christmas day was to be the following Friday. I told her it was a secret and they had to be kept, so she accepted that. We went to C&A on the Damrak and found a special meerschaum corkscrew with sterling silver inlaid for Hans, I also bought another bottle of a 1958 Chateau Lafite to go with it. Then we found a beautiful woolen Jaeger shawl for Anje and I bought a matching Cardigan for her as well. For Miep we went to a home wares shop and bought her a new filter coffee machine, her old one was nearly dying. For her daughter Guda we got a silver bracelet, and for her husband Gerhard a silver fountain pen, he was always writing letters and complaining he didn't have a pen that worked. Just as we were about to walk out of the store, I looked over to the men's clothing dept and I froze. It was Jaap trying on a winter coat! Diny looked at me and said "What on earth is wrong? You have gone pale, are you OK?" It's err, OK my love I just thought I saw someone I used to know" I lied. It definitely was Jaap! What a shock, I'd have to tell Ton when we got back. I recovered my composure and resumed my attention to Diny, she didn't seem to react any further.

We stopped to have a quick bite for lunch, and sat and checked we had got everyone covered as far as presents were concerned, and about 2pm we hopped on a bus back to Diny's place. We got in and wrapped all the presents with the gift wrap we had bought and put the ones for Hans and Anja under the Christmas tree. Diny went upstairs to do something with her hair and I quickly rang Ton to tell him about Jaap. He made no comment just said he would investigate further and for me not to worry.

We had a coffee and sat and planned what would happen on Christmas day. "Will you come round and have Christmas Eve with us?" She asked. "I'd like that, do you have any special traditions?" I asked. "Well, we usually just have a quiet dinner and get to bed early, so it's very relaxed" But Anja and Hans want you to stay so you're with us for Christmas morning" she explained. "That's one time I would prefer to stay in the spare room" I stated. "Yes, that's probably a nice thing to do, but don't expect to be alone all night" She grinned. I laughed back. "Speaking of sex" she interjected "I haven't had you for almost a week, so we better go upstairs and work up an appetite for dinner" "You really are becoming a nymphomaniac" I said. "You complain Senor?" "Not at all" I retorted. It was so good to feel her warm soft body next to mine again and her special smell, I lay there just enjoying looking at her asleep after our sexual exploits.

We had dinner and yet again resumed our lovemaking until the morning. I got up and dressed by 9am and made some breakfast for us both as I wasn't sure how early Anja and Hans would get home. I shouldn't have worried, they didn't get back until 1pm. "Did you have a good evening?" I enquired as they took off their coats. "We had a wonderful time" Anja replied. "Did you two get your shopping done?" we both nodded. "And Robert is staying Christmas Eve mother!" She announced jubilantly. "Good, we can have a really relaxed Christmas then and enjoy" Said Hans. I left them about 3pm after coffee, as I wanted to get clothes ready for Monday and the week, although it was to be a short week, I wanted to get work done and display a responsible attitude, even though most would be out partying.

Chapter 12 – A Happy Christmas

The week flew by I got lots of office work done, and scurried home to Miep early Christmas Eve. I wanted to put their presents under their tree. I told her Diny and I would call round on Christmas morning to enjoy them opening them, she said not to be too early and I promised.

Gerritt had now confirmed the holiday to me and had given me a voucher to present to the travel agent after Christmas to make the final booking arrangements and alongside the voucher, travelers cheques for US$1000! I put this in with Diny's Christmas card. I went round to

Diny's place about 6:30pm and was greeted by Anja who gave me a peck on the cheek and said her welcomes. Diny came down wearing a stunning dress of blue velvet and I stood there admiring her. "You look so beautiful I am speechless" I said. "Well you could give me a kiss instead of standing there like a dumbstruck schoolboy!" She challenged. I gave her a kiss, Hans came in to the room with glasses of champagne and a bottle of Moet & Chandon in an ice bucket. It was delicious! "There is something about the first mouthful of Champagne that is very special" I said. Anja agreed. "Robert, Diny asked me to prepare the spare room in the attic for you as you requested and I have done that, but you know you don't have to stay there if you don't want, Diny has a nice double bed" She stated. I still couldn't get used to the openness of this family, but I countered. "I think it would be only correct and proper for me to stay in the spare room as a guest in your house, I know you accept that Diny and I are now lovers, but there is a time and a place for these things." Anja nodded and said "You should be a politician, that was a very diplomatic answer. "Don't worry mother I'll go and tuck him in!" She said cheekily.

We dined on a roast of Pork, with roasted potatoes and vegetables. After dinner we all had a cognac and coffee Hans offered me a cigar which I accepted, I did not often smoke a cigar and never touched a cigarette, but there is something about the combined aromas of coffee, cognac and cigars that is quite intoxicating in its own way. At around 11:30pm we all decided it was time to sleep and Hans and Anja were the first to say goodnight. Diny and I cuddled up on the couch for 10 minutes. I said I was going to bed and Diny said she would come up to the attic room after she had been to the bathroom. I told her I was not really comfortable about being in bed with her, with her parents in the house. She chided me "So, you are happy to make love when they are not about, but when they really want you to be with me it's not on, is that what you are saying?" "No. darling it's just I'm not used to this open relationship" "Well, you better get used to it, because the bed in the attic is not really made up at all! My mother conned you. Come on, stop protesting and make love to me! It's Christmas!" I followed her up to bed and even checked the attic or "Solder Kamer" as it's called and she was right! Whilst she was in the bathroom I sneaked back downstairs and put the small package with the ring under the tree. I went to the bathroom after her and then snuggled up with her.

I woke up at 08:00 it was still very dark outside, but a street light reflected through the window, and I could see her pretty face in the meagre light. I lay there thinking how lucky could one person be. I stroked her forehead and she opened her eyes and yawned, it was enough to get me aroused again, no sense in getting up too early I thought. "Hans and Anja will probably be doing the same thing we are" she giggled. "So much sex under one roof" I mused.

We all got showered and went down for breakfast around 9:30. Anja had made a wonderful breakfast with cold meats, fresh breads, and lots of coffee. We didn't speak much, "It's amazing how a good night's sleep can make you so hungry isn't it?" Anja grinned. We all smiled back, it confirmed Diny's theory. As we finished breakfast it was decided that it was time to open presents.

Diny gave her mother the present from us first, she put the cardigan on, it fitted perfectly, and she loved the shawl, "I've never had Jaeger stuff before, often looked at it longingly in the shops, It's so well made and high quality, thank you both" She was pleased. Next Hans gave Anja her present from him, it was a beautiful black evening gown made of sheer satin, she went and put it on, and she looked stunning in it! "Wow" I exclaimed, "Hans will have to take you out to dinner to show you off in that" I prompted. "Well, it's funny you say that because here's the second part of the present" Anja opened a small envelope, it was a ticket for the forthcoming New Years Eve ball in Haarlem at the concert hall there. "Thank you so much darling" she kissed him tenderly.

I gave Hans his present from us, the silver inlaid corkscrew was just what he wanted he said. He had been eyeing off a similar one only a week before. Then I gave Diny the small package that was hers. Before I let her open it I announced, "This is a symbol of my friendship for you and the love you have shown me since we met." She tore the wrapping off, and opened the box, Anja came over behind her and watched, they both gasped as the ring let off its brilliance. "It's exquisite, quite the most beautiful piece of jewellery I have ever seen" said Anja. Diny was in tears as she hugged me. "It's just beautiful, thank you my darling" she sobbed. She put it on and Ton had been spot on with the size. "That is just the most beautiful setting" said Hans. "Did Ton make it?" Diny asked. I nodded. "He is just so creative that man, I will ring him and tell him later" she stated.

Diny gave me my present from her, it was a silver photo frame with a photo she had had professionally shot of her, in a blue ball gown and just enough makeup for the photo shoot, it looked like she wasn't really wearing any. It was beautiful and she just looked stunning. It was a great photo I loved it and it would go everywhere with me I told her.

Hans and Anje had a present for me and Diny, as I felt the gift-wrap it felt like a book, I opened it; it was a copy of the Kama Sutra! "Well, you two obviously know the contents of this?" I gave them a cheeky look. "We thought it might be a useful addition to your library" Anja looked directly at me with a smile. "And if I get stuck I can ask you two for advice I suppose?" I queried "Of course!" Said Hans. "We haven't perfected all the positions by a long way, but it's fun practising" he laughed. I must have blushed because Anja leant over to me and said, "Don't worry I won't be setting any exams for you." At least this family had a great sense of humour.

The last present was the card for Diny. "This is also for you and me" I said. She gave me a confused look. Opened it, took a look at the voucher and gasped "Portugal! Mother we are going to Portugal!" Anja and Hans congratulated me on achieving the prize and said they were very proud. I said we should quickly go round to Miep and wish the family a Happy Christmas, and Hans and Anja said they would come too. We put our coats on and walked out into the cold morning air, at least it wasn't raining. Miep was waiting for us with coffee ready, and we watched as they opened their presents. They were all very pleased with the choices.

We sat for a few hours with them just talking and everyone admiring Diny's ring, had a few Jenevers and then went back to Diny's house.

We sat and discussed the past year and some of the momentous things that had happened this past year, the most talked about was the fact that in April the Russians had put Major Yuri Gagarin into space. The world's first astronaut, and we talked about what might happen in the future, maybe a visit to the moon? Or even Mars? Perhaps the old Dan Dare comic strips I used to read in the Eagle comic as a kid weren't so farfetched!

Hans and Anja were good company and we talked about all sorts of topics past and present, they were both knowledgeable and interesting. I was still a bit embarrassed at their present of the book, but started to read it as we had a drink before dinner. It was amazing, I never imagined so many erotic ways to make love existed. Anja came in and saw me reading it, "You need to be a contortionist to achieve some of those positions Robert, don't try too many advanced ones just yet!" I blushed as she said it. "You are not comfortable with our openness I know, but it's much better than treating sex as a forbidden subject like a lot of families do. You will get used to it and realise that we are genuine" She explained. "I'm getting used to it, and I do like being able to discuss anything with you all, and not have secrets" I admitted. I thought of the secret I was keeping from all of them and felt pangs of guilt about hiding it, but Ton had asked me not to tell anyone and I would honour that promise.

Chapter 13 – Reality Bites

The rest of the Christmas days flew by and Diny and I
spent most of it together, and quite a bit of that time in
bed. It was time to return to work all too quickly. I
wended my way up the Uiterweg on my trusty bicycle
promising myself one day I would get my own car. It
was bitterly cold and the Westeinderderplas was
freezing over, the wind was blowing its usual gale,
which didn't make the cycling any easier. I got to work
on time though and Gerritt greeted me with a big smile.
He had his family over from South Holland for the
Christmas and he told me it was a big family gathering,
he seemed pleased to be back in the work routine. All I
could think of was the fact that not two hours ago I had
been snuggled up with Diny and that it would likely be a
week before I had that privilege again. I told Gerritt that
I really should get down to South Holland and Belgium
next week after New Year's Eve, these customers had
not had a visit from us for almost a year, and they
deserved better service. He agreed. So on Wednesday I
would take the car and head south. He told me to take
the car on Tuesday evening and get going early.

New Year's Eve I spent at Diny's house as Hans and
Anje were in Haarlem at the Ball and we had a quiet
night just having dinner together and toasting in the
New Year in bed with a glass of Champagne.

So on Tuesday evening I drove home in the car, an Opel
Kadett. Of course I went to Diny's house first to show
off the fact that I drove a company car, and that I was
going to be away for four days. We bade our farewells

and I went home to Miep and a big plate of vegetable soup, and was asleep by 09:00pm.

The alarm woke me at 6:00am, it was freezing outside, and I scraped the frost off the inside of the window. I gathered my suitcase and belongings together and loaded them into the car. By 7:00am I had eaten breakfast and was driving out of Aalsmeer onto the Grote Weg heading towards Rotterdam and all places south.

As I turned on to the Grote Weg, the first bullet must have punctured the left front tyre because the car took on a mind of its own and careered over the centre strip. The second bullet hit me in the leg, all I felt was a sudden sharp pain and then no feeling at all in my left leg, the bullet must have entered somewhere near the sill of the passenger door. As the car lurched from the centre strip of the road onto the opposite side, all I remember was seeing the front of the truck as it hit the right side of the car then there was just black.

I woke up two days later in hospital, with Ton, Diny and Anja by the bedside. My head was throbbing and I could hardly make out who was there. I suddenly felt very angry and must have let out such a yell, nurses and orderlies came scurrying from everywhere. They gave me a shot of something and I felt calmer. I heard Diny's voice "Oh my darling, it's OK I'm here" I could hear the pain and anxiety in her voice. I felt her hand in mine and felt better. "Never leave me my little Diny, I love you so much!" I pleaded. "Don't worry I will always be here for you" she sobbed.

After a few days of drifting in and out of consciousness, the nurses told me I was very lucky to have survived the crash, the car had ended up underneath the front of the truck. It was fortunate I was on the left side, because the right side had been destroyed completely. I had so many questions in my head, and Ton came in each day to check my progress, but said there would be plenty of time to work out what had happened as soon as I was well again. But my brain wouldn't stop asking the questions.

About a week after the crash I was able to sit up and eat and talk fairly normally. Ton came in about 09:00am, I knew this because it was getting light, and I had no idea what day it was. He said Ralph was here and would I be prepared to see him? I agreed, and was glad that at least someone was interested in all the crazy stuff that was going round in my brain. "Appreciate you seeing me old chap, but there are some things we need to know, did you see anyone prior to the crash?" "No it was dark at that time!" I blurted it out as if he was asking the bleeding obvious. "Well, it was .33mm bullet that took your tyre out, and an armour piercing round that got your leg, so two weapons were involved. Whoever did it was serious" said Ralph. "The armour piercing round was a Russian manufacture, so we think it was Jaap and Kurt or one of their friends. They obviously want you dead" He stated coldly. "Tell me something I don't know!" I announced sarcastically. "Well we know the Russians are close to completing their task of stealing the Blue Streak plans" Ralph said matter of factly. "They also know Kim Philby is about to go to Moscow "I told him. He looked totally shocked "Mr Ellis, you have not told us all you know have you?' He demanded.

Kim Philby, head of the soviet affairs division of MI6 had been dismissed of his duties back in 1956. He had long been suspected of being the third man in the link with Guy Burgess and Donald McClean, these two were British diplomats who had delivered many secret files in the 1940's to the soviets on the west's intentions including the Marshall plan. Kim had laid low for some years and had been assisted by British aristocracy in some cases. Kim was desperate to get to Russia as a safe haven.

"I know all about the deal that was done at Ferry cottage on the Astor estate at Cliveden last year, with minister Profumo being blackmailed as a result of his association with Christine Keeler and a soviet attaché'. And the fact the soviets are also after the Blue Steel project plans, as well as the ECM (Electronic Counter Measures) blueprints for the Vulcan bomber" I almost shouted at him.

"Mr Ellis, you are talking about subject matter that even I know nothing about here, where did you get this information?' Ralph demanded. "When Jaap left his briefcase in my room to take the diamonds to the meeting, there were documents with all this information in the secret compartment in the base, I looked at them and memorised them, they were in German. He must have come back after I left and realised he had left them and switched the briefcases back, transferring the stones back into his briefcase" I explained. "Mr Ellis, I am going to give you protective custody as of now in this hospital, until I verify some of this" He was obviously flustered at information he did not understand.

A half hour later an armed British soldier sporting an SAS red beret was standing at the base of my bed. Two hours later, Ralph reappeared with another man who called himself Commander Lewers, the commander explained he was with British intelligence and would I explain what I had seen in the documents in the briefcase. He had a tape recorder with him, and I told him in English and German exactly what the contents of the papers were. I told him that whilst Burgess & McClean were long gone. Philby was now trying to get to the protection of the soviets before his story was totally blown. A deal had been agreed to with Profumo that the Keeler affair as well as the involvement with the soviet attaché' would be hushed up for as long as possible, in exchange Philby would be left alone, allowing him to quietly disappear to the USSR. He went white when I mentioned the Blue Steel and ECM projects. I also explained there were names in the document of senior staff in the MOD who were being bribed with gifts supposedly from suppliers, to gain information about these projects. "Mr Ellis, I must now place you under the highest level of secrecy, you are not to mention to anyone about these matters, do you understand?" "Yes of course Commander" I replied.

Diny came to visit me that evening and was alarmed at the soldier at the foot of my bed. "What the hell is this all about?' She pleaded. "It's routine darling, as I've told you my father works for the government, any family member involved in an accident gets protection as a matter of course" I lied to her what I had agreed with Commander Lewers before, having told him about my romantic involvement.

My story was verified the next day by a visit from Ralph and Commander Lewers, they told me the names of the staff in the document were some that were already under suspicion, and others they had no idea were involved until now. He told me to be very careful once I was discharged from hospital and that whilst they could provide some protection for me, it was not certain I could be covered all the time. He asked me if I wanted to quit and go home. I replied that I wanted to see this through.

Commander Lewers continued, "OK Mr Ellis, what I am now going to tell you is of the highest classification in terms of secrecy, but you need to know the full story in order to help us. The Russians as you may know are attempting to build an ICBM capable of delivering a nuclear warhead anywhere in Europe and possibly the East Coast of the USA. After what happened off Cuba last year the Americans are concerned as much as we are that they do not succeed. Our guidance system is what they are after, their system is primitive and does not work well. In several days time the first test of the Blue Streak will take place at Woomera, a remote testing site in South Australia. We have brought the project forward over a year, it was originally scheduled for June next year but because of the way the Russians are behaving. They will want to get their hands on data from those tests as soon as they can. We are going to feed dummy and false data to certain depts in the MOD to try and trace where the leaks are. You can expect heightened activity from our friends here at that time. We expect more diamonds to be exchanged to pay for the bribes. The British government has been severely embarrassed in recent times by certain defections and we have to show to the Yanks that we are serious and can be trusted to keep classified data safe" I nodded. "What we want you to do is to report all and any activity that may appear to have a bearing on when and where money or stones will change hands. Do not, I repeat do not, try and extract information. Just report what you see and hear, we are going to give you an encryption device that will enable you to talk via any phone in a secure way to Ton, he in turn will relay info to us, do you understand all this?" I nodded again. "We expect that you will go about your job activities in a normal way so as not arouse any suspicion" "What do I do about the crash, and the trip to Belgium?" I asked. It seemed strange that Gerritt had not paid me a visit. "Gerritt is one of our agents planted many years back to monitor Jaap and Kurt, he knows everything he needs to know about what is going on, but you must not talk to him about anything, we think there is a planted agent at the business to monitor him." Commander Lewers went on to explain that the reason Gerritt had taken me out to dinner was to make sure I could be trusted and was mature enough to handle this situation. "No offense Mr Ellis, but Her Majesty's Government does not take lightly to entrusting an 18 year old young man with national secrets, we had to make sure you could keep your mouth shut." Ralph explained there would be a replacement car once I was out of hospital, and that I should proceed to Belgium as planned. They would tell a false story about the crash to try and make the other side believe they had got the wrong vehicle.

They left and Diny came in looking very confused. "What was that all about?" she queried. "Oh it was people from the British Government just making sure I was OK, so they can report back to home" I fibbed. Diny accepted the explanation, and we talked about what we would do once I got back from Belgium.

Chapter 14 - The other side of the Diamond

It was fully a week before I could leave hospital, Diny, bless her had stayed almost all the time by my side. She looked drained and exhausted the day I left the hospital with her, clutching my arm as if I was going to escape from her and never come back if she let go.

We went back to her parents place. They insisted I should stay a few days before going back to work, but I wanted to get on the road, have some time to myself and ponder what the next move would be in this amazing scenario I had managed to implant myself into.

I couldn't stop Diny and Anya from fussing around me and must confess it was pretty nice! After two days I was up and about and told Diny I would head off in the morning to Belgium, she wasn't sure I was up to it but decided not to argue the point. The next morning I got into the replacement Opel Kadett and drove off with some considerable nervousness, and a feeling of apprehension about having to drive past the same spot I had been shot at only two weeks before. Prior to driving off I had checked the glove box as instructed by Ralph who had called by Diny's place a day before. In the compartment there was a small black bakelite object about the size of a cigarette packet, it had a series of slits on one side and a round holed aperture on the other. I had been told that when held over a phone mouthpiece I could speak into it and it would encode my voice, so that anyone tapping into a conversation would only hear white noise. However, the recipient on the other end of the line with a similar device, would hear my voice perfectly. This really was James Bond stuff! All I needed now was the DB6! I recalled as I drove towards Rotterdam, the Ian Fleming books that I had eagerly devoured at college, and thought of what "Q" might think of my phone scrambler.

The whole situation seemed to me to be preposterous, what on earth could I do now to further solve the mystery of where Jaap and Kurt were, who had arranged the shooting? What was going to go wrong next? What would happen to the diamonds I had still under the bed at Hadleystraat? Would they want them back? It wasn't difficult to imagine they would.

My first stop was to be Antwerp and Ton had arranged for me to stay at a fellow diamond cutter and polishers house instead of a hotel, he thought that would be more secure and less likely to be tracked. I drove into the historic city and enjoyed its old world charm as I approached the centre of the city. As I drove into town, I pondered on one piece of information I had sighted in Jaap's briefcase that I had not told Commander Lewers about, mainly because I wasn't sure of its relevance and what it was about. The document mentioned "Echelon" and some kind of interception of data. It didn't make sense but until I knew more I was going to keep it to myself.

Ton had arranged for me to stay with a friend of his also a diamond merchant, Jean-Paul Hermans a Flemish speaking resident of Antwerp, but of dual parentage. His mother was French and his father a Walloon of fiercely Flemish character.

Belgium is a constant battleground between French and Flemish (a direct dialect of Dutch) speaking people, and to an outsider it seems the country cannot decide which it belongs to, as there are constant tirades in the press and on the radio as to which should be the dominant language. However, most of the time the population gets on with the business of surviving and the country is really quite wealthy.

Jean-Paul greeted me at the door of his narrow house situated in a cobbled street not far from the centre of town. He ushered me in and immediately showed me to the spare room, where I dumped my suitcase. He showed me to the Lounge room and without asking poured me a Genever, he looked tired and weary, and I told him I would only be staying a few days and how very nice it was of him to offer accommodation. He said it was not a problem and would I like to go down the street with him and share a meal at the local café? I was starving and gladly agreed to the proposition. We downed our Genever's and walked out of the house.

As we walked we discussed diamonds and how they had been an integral part of the Antwerp economy for many years. We sat down in the café and ordered another round of Genever, this time I ordered the old genever as I preferred it. Jean-Paul leant across to me and said "I wanted to come here, as I think the house is bugged" I must have looked very confused, "I know Ton is trying to help detect the diamond smugglers" He confided. I concluded Ton must have spun a story about counterfeit stones and how they were being smuggled from Africa.

"They have my wife!" He broke into tears as he said this. Oh God! I thought, what next? "Tell me what happened?" I queried. "Last night they came and knocked on the door while we were having dinner, and took her away, and said I should ring a number once you arrived" I sat transfixed. "I rang Ton and he said he would take care of it and not to ring the number at any cost" "Oh my God I am so sorry to have got you involved in this" I pleaded. He held up a hand and said "It's OK I was in the resistance at the end of the war and I know what it's like to be under pressure."

I must have looked shocked, because he went on, "I know where the stones are from and who is bringing them in, they are being brought in by flight crew working for SABENA, and they get paid for it. I also know they are being taken from here to Amsterdam after being given a "rough" cut and a false certificate of authenticity, so when they get to Amsterdam, most dealers don't know where they are from and process them into the market. Skilled people like Ton can see they are not quota stock and smell a rat, but other's either don't care or don't know"

He continued "I have seen some of these stones, and they are of high grade, with very few inclusions, and usually they are D rated stones or at the very least F. Their clarity is often WS1 or 2, and carat weight is often

.5 to 1 carat so as not to arouse the suspicion that larger stones would."

"What is happening to your wife?" I queried. "Ton said he was negotiating with the people that took her, and asked that you ring him once I had explained all this." I went to the back of the café to the phone, took the decoder out of my pocket and rang Ton, "Ton, what on earth is this about?" I demanded. "Robert, don't worry, we arranged for his wife to be taken into safe custody last night, we have her although Jean-Paul thinks she was taken by the opposition." "As she would have been if we had not got there first" I tried to interrupt. "Listen carefully to me and say nothing, after you have had a meal there, go and get your suitcase and a car will pick you up, you will be taken to a safe place" Ton hung up, I was totally confused by now.

I went back to the table and Jean-Paul had already ordered a bottle of St Estephe` and was pouring it. "Have a look at the menu it's very good" He exclaimed as if we were just out for a good dinner and a boys night out. He smiled "Don't worry Robert it will all be OK, let's enjoy our meal, you are paying!"

We ate very well, I had a sole meunier as a starter and a pork cutlet for mains. Jean-Paul had oysters and a steak for mains, we had a few cognacs after with coffee, and I paid the bill, noting it was not as expensive as I had expected. We walked back to his house, I got my bag and a car drew up outside and I got in without having a chance to say goodbye to Jean-Paul.

As I got into the car Commander Lewers greeted me from the opposite side rear seat, leant over to me and stuck a needle in my arm. I woke up in a room that had no furnishings except for a chair, nothing on the walls, bare polished wood floors, and Commander Lewers was sitting in the chair opposite smiling at me. His smile gave me a feeling of great fear.

"Mr Ellis, you have not been entirely truthful with us have you?" He demanded. "I have no idea what you are talking about!" I replied curtly. "Tell me what else you saw on the papers in the briefcase?" I was still groggy from whatever he had injected me with. "I have no idea what you are on about" I replied. The Commander was clearly in no mood to compromise. "Did you see anything that mentioned Echelon?" He asked. I was suspicious, so replied in the negative. "Mr Ellis we are not going to tolerate any kind of subplots from you or anyone in this matter, do you understand?' Before I had a chance to respond the door burst open and an SAS soldier shot Commander Lewers in the head and he fell to the floor, his feet rattled on the bare boards and his mouth poured blood as he lay there gasping his final breaths. By now I was terrified and had no idea what was going on.

Ralph followed the SAS soldier into the room and looked at me. "Mr Ellis, you have done well, we didn't expect you to be so professional!" He announced. "I have no idea what the bloody hell is going on here!" I screamed, "Would you please, once and for all tell me where I am and what this is all about!" I was almost hysterical by now.

Ralph took me out of the room and down a flight of stairs to a waiting car, he said nothing, and we drove in silence a few blocks and arrived outside a grey building with large oak doors. He opened the door and showed me in, we went to an office and he sat me down. "Mr Ellis, I will now tell you exactly what is going on and you will realise then precisely why all this has taken place"

"We got wind of an attempt to kill you tonight and also to abduct the wife of Jean-Paul. Our combatants in this affair had planned to use her as a hostage and use that leverage to obtain certain concessions from us with regard to some of the people that are under suspicion in the various Government departments we previously talked about. We also discovered only hours ago that Commander Lewers was in fact a plant as well. The car we sent to pick you up was not the one that you got into, once we realised Lewers had you we knew where to come"

"I also must tell you that the Echelon name that Commander Lewers mentioned is in fact a worldwide communication network set up by the USA and UK as far back as 1947, to enable the rapid and secure transmission of confidential data. We have known for some months that this system has been compromised and therefore we have been deliberately sending false data via this system and the real data has been sent via a secure telex system instead, until we can change the encryption method to make it secure again."

I sat there with my mouth open like some village idiot. "You did particularly well in trying to tell Lewers you had no idea what he was talking about, as that room was bugged and they now think their interception of the code is safe"

Ralph went over to a cabinet and poured two large cognacs into brandy balloons, and gave me one. "You need this Mr Ellis and you have certainly earned it" He said with a smile on his face. "You will stay here tonight, the place is guarded by many SAS troops and you can get a good night's sleep, we will continue this de-brief in the morning."

I did not sleep well, there were so many things revolving around in my brain, so many unanswered questions. I felt as though I was going to crack under the pressure. In the morning Ralph came after I had showered and invited me to have breakfast with him. We went downstairs to a room with a table set for three, and as we entered the room my father stepped from the other side of a desk and said "I hope you now realise what you are involved with? Because, I sure as hell don't like it!" Ralph beckoned him to be quiet. "No! I will say what I think! I believe it was reckless and foolish to involve him in the first place, and he certainly won't stand up to the pressure for long!" This made me bristle, if there was one thing that annoyed the hell out of me was my own father putting me down, especially in front of others. "Now look here!" I bellowed. "There have been moments in all this that I have felt frightened, and confused and even at the point of giving up. But one thing I do know is that I have never thought this was reckless, foolish or wrong. There are clearly forces at work here that want to do harm to our allies and us. I don't profess to understand it all, but one thing I do know is that if I can in some small way help to thwart what they are trying to do, then I will do it and am prepared to put my life on the line if necessary!"

"Well Mr Ellis you appear to have misjudged your son, he is clearly committed to this cause, and obviously we must use his patriotic attitude to further our cause "Ralph smirked. "I am not happy with your patronising demeanour towards me either Ralph." I snarled. " While we are airing our dirty linen. I believe you have deliberately lured me into this by telling me just enough to keep me interested, but not enough to keep me from being as safe as I could have been had I known more about what was going on"

"Mr Ellis I am not in the habit of taking criticism from 18 year olds still wet behind their ears! However I will concede we have not told you everything because we felt it was in your own interests. From now on there will be no vetting of information, you already know more than most cabinet ministers anyway" Ralph seemed a bit hurt by my outburst.

Ralph continued, "I will now brief you with as much as I am permitted to know, we do not know what has happened to Jaap and Kurt, but we believe they killed two KGB agents back in Hamburg and planted false documents on them. We also know as I mentioned before, the Russians have somehow decrypted the Echelon code and until we can re-code the entire system we are merely sending false data around the network. Lewers was not privy to this information so you did well in making him think it was safe, even though he is dead, the conversation was overheard by others who will think the system is still alive. This does not mean however that we are out of the woods, we still have moles in Whitehall feeding data back to Moscow, and it will take some time to weed them out. The threat is still very high and the first Blue Streak launch takes place within the next 48hrs at Woomera. They will be expecting a flurry of data on the network after it has taken place and we will not disappoint them. Meantime, we still know that more diamonds are being channeled through the system, large quantities, so they are up to something more than regular payments to moles. We need to find out what it is, and how to stop it. By the way in case you are wondering why Lewers picked you up and not us, the car and driver that was supposed to meet you was intercepted and the driver killed just a block away from where you were collected."

I sat there drawing a deep breath, and considering how lucky I was to be alive. "Ralph I have a gut feeling that the KGB is trying to overthrow a European government" Ralph looked horrified at me. "What on earth makes you think that!?" He demanded. "When I was on the ferry from Harwich, I overheard them say that what they were doing would change the face of Europe forever. It just occurred to me that perhaps they not only want our ICBM data, but our sovereignty too!" "Hmmm, perhaps they are up to schemes that would destabilise the NATO organisation or some such plan" Ralph pondered. "Thank you, for your theory Robert, we will investigate some possible scenarios. That is most helpful"

We sat and ate breakfast discussing the rationale behind Russia's attempt to launch its own ICBM and what they might be up to in order to change the equilibrium between East and West. We did not come up with answers but all three of us agreed we had to watch out for anything that might give a clue as to what they might have planned.

I actually had 15 minutes alone with my father before he left and that may have changed our relationship dramatically. He told me he was very proud of what I was doing and that he was sorry for his criticism of me in the past. But he did caution me that I was trading my life for what I believed in and that he wasn't sure I really understood what that meant. I told him I was not so sure about anything anymore, but that my country had so far given me a great life and I was prepared to fight to keep it that way. Later when I had time to think about this, it made me shudder with fear as to what was around the corner.

Chapter 15 The Going Gets Tough

That afternoon I actually went and did sales calls so as to appear normal, I picked up a few orders and for a few hours felt like a normal person going about their job. Around 5:30 in evening I returned to the grey building I had christened "The Compound" as instructed by Ralph. Neither he nor my father were to be seen, but the staff were very careful to look after me and not to talk to me, it was all very clinical. I ordered a club sandwich and coffee and was in bed by 8:30pm and fell asleep very quickly. I awoke at 06:00 and shaved and showered, went down to the lounge where breakfast was served, Ralph was there sitting smugly with a cup of coffee,

"Oh, how I detest this man!" I thought. "Good morning Robert!" he greeted me. "We have investigated your theory about the possibility of governments being under threat and cannot come up with any trace of evidence, however we would appreciate you relaying any further info you may come across"

"I will certainly do that Ralph" I confirmed. "Ralph, it's time to put the record straight. I get the feeling you do not like me, let me tell you I like you even less. You have obviously spent your life climbing the government ladder and brown nosing your way into a cushy little job that allows you to order other people about, and allows you to also feel you are part of the MI6 hierarchy. Let me say as a civilian I do not trust you or appreciate your smug attitude to what has unfolded in the past weeks. I find your attitude to the demise of certain people offensive, but I also recognise that you are a senior officer by rank, and will do as you ask."

"Thank you for your frankness Robert, I understand that, I do not asked to be liked, it's part of the job and I think it is good that we have a professional relationship that allows us to get on with the sordid job we have to do"

Suddenly I felt guilty about getting stuck into him that way, maybe he wasn't a bad guy after all. "Ralph, maybe in another life we would have a better understanding of each other, I get the feeling you do not always like what you do?" "Robert none of us like what we do in this business, but we are trained not to question orders and you must do the same, take the emotion out of what you do, but preserve the passion" He chided.

After breakfast Ralph briefed me on the people that were under suspicion back in UK, in case their names came up in conversations I might overhear. I went out and did a full day's sales calls without any interruptions. Arriving back at "The Compound" around 5pm.

The next day I drove back to the border and enjoyed the drive across the wintry flat landscape that is South Holland, taking the main road past Rotterdam and arriving home to Miep by around 4pm, it was already dark and I was glad to see her smiling face. "Diny wants you call her" she announced as I walked in to the house. "Ask her over to share some soup if you like" she volunteered. I rang her and she was at the front door within minutes, we kissed and she told me she had missed me so much, and was glad I was home safe. It was so good to hold her and smell her and feel her body next to mine.

We sat and ate Miep's vegetable soup and homemade bread, laughing and telling each other how the week had gone. Miep suggested that as it was very cold out Diny should stay, with a twinkle in her eye she told me it was alright that Diny stayed with me. Diny did not object and neither did I, it was 9:30pm and we all decided it was time to turn in for the night as we all had busy days tomorrow.

Diny came up the stairs behind me and we went into my room. I stood and held her hand, looked at her in light from the street coming through the window, her lovely pale soft skin reflected in the light, and I knew this was one special girl in my life. "Diny, I do love you so much" "I love you too Robert" she was so committed in the way she said that. We just held each other and kissed, then got undressed without a word spoken and held each other's naked bodies in bed for what seemed like ages, then made long slow love and fell into a wonderful deep sleep.

The next morning Diny went to the university and I went to work. It was a strange day, I didn't speak much to anybody and everyone seemed to accept my silence. I processed a number of repeat orders from Berlin and also the orders I had collected in Belgium. It was all very routine and I felt somewhat uneasy that everything seemed normal.

I went home to Miep and her family and enjoyed another great "Erwtensoup" for dinner. After, I went round to Diny's place, she had only just got home and looked tired, she had her dinner whilst I talked to her. She looked at her ring and smiled to me, "I do love this Robert, it's so special" I smiled and enjoyed her radiance glowing back at me.

"Diny, I need to tell you something, it is not easy to do this but, all is not as it may seem in my life right now. I am involved in a situation that I cannot tell you everything about, but I will tell you as much as I am able. My father is in the Ministry of Defence as you know in England, and there are things going on here that require me to report back to his department, it is of high importance to not only the British government but to many European governments as well"

Diny looked puzzled at my half baked story "So that is why there were military people at the hospital and why you couldn't tell me anything?" "Yes my love it is very complex, and I don't want to tell you anything that could place you in danger, but you need to understand I'm doing it for what I believe in Diny".

She seemed to accept my crazy story and I was glad I had told her something at least. We went to the front room to join Anje and Hans watching TV. It was already January 15th and the news was on, the main story was Alabama's new Governor, George Wallace, giving his inauguration speech, during which he shouted, "Segregation no! Segregation tomorrow! Segregation forever!" The deep south of America was having racial problems, his idea was to keep the blacks and whites apart to prevent violence erupting.

I walked back home wondering whether I had done the wrong thing telling Diny, and maybe creating more concern in her mind rather than giving her a reason to understand what on earth was going on.

I think in the light of the grey morning the following day, cycling my way to work, I was feeling that I had done the wrong thing in even confiding the smallest detail of my story to Diny. She probably didn't believe me anyway, it was such a flimsy story. On the other hand maybe I was just thinking of the guilt I was feeling in not being able to tell her the full story.

My thoughts were interrupted by the voice of Ton who had appeared in a car beside me. "We need to talk

Robert" he demanded, it was not a request. I got off my bike and he pointed to De Uil Café across the canal. We got on to the chain pulled ferry and made our way into the glass fronted lounge, ordered two coffees and sat down at one of the heavily clothed tables. Dirk the waiter brought our coffees with a small biscuit and the usual Koffiemelk. The Dutch have special creamy milk they put in their coffee, I drink mine black.

"Robert, your theory about the Russians wanting to destabilise the European equilibrium has caused a deal of concern in Whitehall, they think there may be some truth in your theory, what exactly do you think?" He asked. "I don't really know what may be unfolding Ton, I just have this feeling that all the trouble they are taking to raise funds from clandestine stones is just a cover for something bigger. I mean if they really wanted just enough cash to pay for some secrets, they could flog off some petty jewels from the Kremlin and get more than they are getting from this". I continued my crazy thoughts, "Whilst I think the stealing of Blue Streak and the rest of the arsenal of top secret projects the British government may be working on is serious. I also think they have greater aspirations as to their role in Europe. They do not like being poor and to some extent abhor the fact that the rest of Europe consider them second tier relatives, it is not acceptable that they are on the back foot and that Britain and US are calling the shots."

Ton, sat silent and absorbed my rantings, " Robert, you may have a very valid theory, you are right when you say the Russians would be better off with a destabilised Europe, there are moves afoot to set up a European Union that would eclipse the United States in economic power. The Russians feel they may be watching the demise of their Socialist way of life, and because the hierarchy live so well from the system, they don't want to lose the control they have. A united Europe would pose a great threat to their system."

Ton asked me to keep my ears open to any further information I may come across, and he would pass on my thoughts. I mused as I continued on to work, what if I'm wrong? What if my theory is total nonsense? Would I be locked up for having mad theories, thrown in an asylum for the insane, never to see the light of day again because of my crazy thoughts? Probably I thought, that's likely what the British government would do.

The rest of the day was routine, nobody bothered me much. More orders from Berlin and also Belgium now were to be processed and I got through them working out in my head roughly how much commission it would give me. I would soon have enough money to look after Diny and myself quite well. Then as I sat at my desk, I thought of the diamonds that still sat in the briefcase under my bed! What would I do if they suddenly became mine by virtue of the three month waiting period? To sell them via Ton or just put them in a safe deposit and forget them? It was only a few weeks to wait until they were legally mine. I resolved to consult Ton about them.

I cycled home, it was getting cold and the wind was adding to the chill factor. As I turned off the Aalsmeerderweg a car drew alongside and nearly knocked me off my bike. I was grabbed from behind and dragged into the car a black cloth placed over my eyes so I had no idea who had grabbed me. "Robert, we need to talk to you" The voice of Jaap boomed at me, he sounded angry. The blindfold was removed, I was confronted by the face of Jaap on my left and Kurt on my right. "What the hell is this all about?" I stammered, "I thought you guys were dead!" "No Robert, just away for a while" Kurt calmly reassured. "You have done well, you have not told anyone about our story" Jaap congratulated me. "But, now we need your help, and you must listen very carefully to what I have to tell you, because you are now involved whether you like it or not, and we must trust you. Back in September last year, on the 29th to be precise, President Krushchev sent a letter to President Kennedy from his dacha at the Black Sea. He outlined his concern about the Presidents television address of July 3rd, calling it belligerent in nature, and likely to propel the destiny of the world into directions that it would not wish to be placed. He also referred to meetings with Prime Minister Fanfani of Italy, former PM of France Paul Reynaud and Mr Spaak of the Belgian government. He seemed to believe that these people were conspiring against the USSR to affect the peace equilibrium. As a result, in this letter Chairman Krushchev questioned the dilemma facing the guarantees of West Berlin, and how it could be resolved, he suggested that the occupation of West Berlin by the allies must be eliminated. He asked that Andrei Gromyko and Dean Rusk meet and discuss options." Shortly after this the Cuban missile crisis made that meeting impossibility.

"What has all this to do with us?" I asked. "Robert, we are working to resolve this situation decisively under orders from our KGB superiors, we are to take out these heads of state with hired contractors and create such turmoil in Europe that they will not notice our taking over West Berlin and solving this problem once and forever!" Kurt sounded very agitated as he said this.

"My god you are going to assassinate the heads of government of Italy, Belgium and France?" My head was reeling. "Also, the heads of state of the United Kingdom, and Spain" Jaap confirmed. "You are going to do all this?" "We are not going to do it Robert, but others are employed to perform these duties" Kurt said coldly. "I see, but where do we come in? I still am not clear about that." I questioned. Jaap continued, "The diamonds we have been accumulating are going to pay for this, we need you to courier these stones to an address in Paris later this month. The stones will then be distributed along with orders to the contractors, and they will carry out their tasks in early April, this will result in chaos for a short while, allowing Russian troops to enter Berlin and unite the city once and for all." "But won't the US and Britain try to retaliate?" I questioned. " We have acquired plans of the ICBM that Britain has designed and are about to test fire a few days from now in Australia, Russia will threaten to use this weapon against its own designers if they retaliate" Kurt explained.

"Robert we need you to take these stones to Paris, because they know us and we would not get past customs, but you are a legitimate sales person going about your business, less likely to be suspected" Jaap went on. "What if I refuse to do this? " I retorted. "Then your beloved Diny and her family will die!" Kurt said coldly. "I see, then I will have to do this, although it terrifies me to be involved" I wanted them to feel they had me cornered. "Good, then we will prepare the stones and arrange for you to courier them" Kurt confirmed. "You will go about your work as normal and we will contact you again once everything is ready" said Kurt.

Chapter 16 – Bloody Oath!

Woomera, South Australia is about 2.5 hrs drive from Port Augusta on the dirt road that is the Stuart Highway. Greg Brereton was driving his 1958 FC Holden "Ute" on that highway heading for Coober Pedy as his ultimate destination, but the service station at the Woomera turnoff was where he would overnight and have a meal. About 30 minutes out from Port Augusta with the majestic Flinders Ranges on his rear right side now disappearing into the horizon and the scrub on both sides thinning to the occasional clump of saltbush and the odd cattle grid (there are 49 between Port Augusta and Coober Pedy) keeping him from falling asleep as the Ute rumbled across them.

It was hot in January! 45c and with the windows down the dust blinded Greg from time to time. "Bloody Oath, I'm looking forward to a few cold beers tonight" he mumbled to himself. A small climbing turn in the road and he was suddenly presented with a large truck right in front of him with 3 police cars behind it, the truck was a flatbed with large crates overhanging the sides of the trailer on it, and no distinguishing marks on either the truck or crates. "Christ! What the hell is going on here?" Greg muttered. He slowed down behind the police cars and started to calculate in his mind how much longer this would delay him. One of the police cars slowed down and motioned him to stop, he did so and both vehicles came to a stop in the dusty side margin of the road, a police officer got out of his car and strode towards Greg. "Sorry blue, the bloody truck's got so much overhang and it only does 20 miles an hour, we had to escort it, it's only going as far as Woomera, where are you going?" The officer asked. Greg explained he was going to stay at the Pimba service station and go on to Coober Pedy the next day. "Well, let's see if we can get you past this bloody rig mate, it's all the flaming poms fault, they are doing some machinery testing up there and this is all their gear, we had to escort it from Port Adelaide for the past two days and it's a pain in the arse" the officer seemed totally pissed off about the whole thing.

Greg smiled as thought about the poor police officers having to escort this unmarked load at 20 miles per hour, and how he thought he had a tough time ferrying machine parts up to Coober Pedy, but these guys have it worse!

Greg was waved on past the huge load by the police and was just about to pass the cab of the prime mover when he noticed that the arm protruding from the window was a military uniform and on second glance the uniform displayed the pips of a British army officer, as he drove on past the convoy he looked back to see several army uniforms in the cab, further up the road, he passed a Land Rover that also had British military markings. So, the police officer was not joking Greg mused, bloody poms he thought, what on earth are they doing in the outback of Australia?

At exactly 102 kms north of Port Augusta Greg came up to the junction in the road at Glendambo, the Pimba roadhouse, where you decide to go on to Coober Pedy and continue the torturous journey past the vast salt lakes shimmering in the distance from the road, or stop and stay at the meagre accommodation offered at the roadhouse. As a regular user of the road Greg knew it was not a good idea to venture on this road after dusk, the chance of hitting a kangaroo or other nocturnal beast was too high. So the prospect of a cold beer or four and a good meal and maybe a bit of conversation with the truckies was much more attractive.

Pimba roadhouse is basic accommodation but the rooms have fans and the beds are reasonably comfortable. The bar and restaurant however serve the best steaks and cold beer in the area mainly because it is the only bar and restaurant within 2-3 hours drive of anywhere! Woomera 20 minutes down the road is a closed area for the public and is for military personnel only and although they also have accommodation and the usual creature comforts that military personnel enjoy it is not considered an option for anyone other than authorised people.

Greg parked his Ute and walked to the main entrance, checked in at the counter, got the key to his room, dumped his roll of belongings on the bed and went straight to the bar. Australian beer is to be enjoyed very cold and drunk from glasses that are kept in the chiller, thus for Greg the feel of the cold glass in his hand and the flow of chilled amber fluid down his gullet was one of pure delight. He hardly noticed anyone else in the bar until he ordered his second glass, then he looked around, there were a couple of guys who regularly haul goods to Alice Springs and beyond at the far end of the bar that he recognised, and there was one guy on his own downing a beer about 5 feet away, apart from that it was empty. He acknowledged the guy on his own, walked down to where he was sitting at the bar and asked his name, they shook hands, Stefan he told Greg in a heavy accent, Greg asked him where he was from and he said Adelaide, "no, I mean what country you from?" Stefan said he was from Ukraine originally, but now he was going to Coober Pedy to seek his fortune in opals. Greg said it was a tough business, and Stefan said he had friends there that already had struck some good colour.

After a few more beers Greg and Stefan were talking like old friends, and Greg was telling Stefan about the huge truck load he had encountered earlier, Stefan seemed interested so Greg went on about the cops and the military uniforms, and the overhanging load. Stefan said it was the third load this week that had gone into Woomera, Greg thought it strange that Stefan knew this but he just said he had been here a few extra days while his car got fixed and he noticed these loads going past. Greg moved on the conversation to Aussie rules football and the Grand Final in Melbourne in September and how he thought Hawthorn stood a great chance of getting into the final series, they discussed the merits of David Parkin as a back at Hawthorn, Greg had been a Hawthorn fan for years, and it was great to find someone who shared his interest. Stefan and Greg ordered dinner and shared a few more beers before going to bed.

In the morning the harsh light of the outback day woke Greg at 5:30am and he decided to have a shower and get an early start for the 5 hour drive to Coober Pedy. He went to the restaurant and ordered a full breakfast with lambs fry and bacon, to set him up for the rest of the day. He drove out of the Pimba Roadhouse at 7:30am and started his journey northwards. About half an hour out just before the first of the salt lakes come into view, Greg noticed a white flash off to the right in his peripheral vision, he slowed down and looked at the trail of a rocket that seemed to have amazing speed as it rushed upwards into the clear blue sky and after about 50 seconds had disappeared into the sky leaving nothing but a few puffs of its contrail. Greg mused whether that had been part of what the police officer had told him the poms were up to. He was right, it had been the first successful launch of Blue Streak , there were more launches to come and the boxes Greg saw on the truck were part of the second launch.

He drove on and about 2 miles further up the road, he came across Stefan packing stuff into a car and a double axle trailer, he stopped to see if he could help. Stefan told him it was OK he could manage, but Greg was curious as to why he would be out here so early. So he got out and walked over to Stefan, Stefan pulled out a Luger hand gun and shot Greg dead on the spot. Stefan pulled the body into the scrub and drove Greg's Ute into the scrub so it could not be seen from the road.

Stefan drove off after finishing his packing and headed south, it would be 3 days before anyone discovered Greg's body and his Ute after being reported late arriving in Coober Pedy. And Stefan by then was well on his way via Adelaide and Sydney back to Europe never to be seen again. Not however before sending a package with photos and a handwritten report of what he had seen to the Soviet Embassy in Canberra. Stefan, if that indeed was his name, had been a sleeper for the soviets staying put for a number of years, and now had left Australia. The contents of his package, was already received via the diplomatic bag at KGB headquarters in Moscow within 3 days. This test of the Blue Streak was never documented and the first official record still shows June 1964 as the first.

Chapter 17 - What the hell?

I stepped off the train on platform 2 at Gare Du Nord and made my way out to the taxi rank, after about 10 mins of waiting I got into a Citroen taxi and asked the driver to take me to Hotel Scribe in Rue Scribe. Rue Scribe is in the Opera area of Paris, just down the road is Boulevard Du Cappucines and some great restaurants. As it was early evening I checked in and walked from my hotel past The Grand Hotel and across the busy boulevard, passing the Scandinavian Airlines office, I flagged down a taxi that took me to a restaurant that had been recommended by Gerritt, Le Jeroboam. This restaurant has a unique style, you can get a glass of fine vintage wine to suit each course, instead of ordering a single bottle. So, I had a glass of wonderfully crisp Pouilly Fume with my Sole Meuniere as a starter and a great Chateau Latour with my filet of beef as a main course, followed inevitably by another glass with an assorted platter of cheeses.

France, to my mind has some of the world's greatest cheeses, apart from the obvious Brie and Camembert. Pont Levecque, Rocquefort, Bresse Bleu, and Savoyarde from the cool Savoy mountain areas bordering Switzerland, are some of the most tantalizing cheeses in the world, having promised Gerritt I would enjoy at least one night in Paris at his expense, who was I to argue!

The only thing missing from this gastronomic feast was my beloved Diny, but I promised myself I would bring her here one day. I finished off the evening with a black coffee and a glass of a 20 year old Cles Des Ducs Armagnac. I got a taxi back to the Hotel feeling pretty inebriated and relaxed, I was enjoying the calm and normality of being a normal human being.

I slept well, and woke at 6:30 am with a start from the shrill beep of the alarm clock. Showered, dressed, and went down to the restaurant for breakfast, as I entered Ralph grabbed me by the arm and escorted me to a table he had already reserved. "We need to talk!" He demanded.

We sat at a window table and with 2 tables between anyone else, Ralph explained that the Woomera test firing had successfully taken place but that the Australian ASIO office had informed them they thought the operation had been compromised by someone on the ground sending data back to the Russians. This didn't really mean much to me at that moment, but I nodded and agreed with Ralph that it complicated the issue.

Ralph said it was going to be a fairly risky time ahead and that I should think twice before making any moves on my own. He also confided that several people back at the Ministry had been taken into custody. The Russians would not be happy about that he warned. "Ralph just what the hell is going on? I mean here we are, knowing the Russians are trying to take out the major heads of state in 5 or 6 countries and we seem powerless to stop it?" Ralph smiled "It is not for us to question or worry, Robert there are plans in place now to cope with the possible outcomes, all we need to do is keep track of what is happening and report back". "Now let's talk about other matters". It was Ralph's way of closing a conversation he no longer wished to pursue.

He asked me what I thought was going to happen and how it might play out. I told him quite frankly I had no idea at this point, but knew I would be contacted as to where the stones were to be left and that was all. Ralph told me to phone Ton using the scrambler once the drop had been made and I acknowledged the instruction. Ralph finished his coffee and left.

After breakfast I went back to my room and got my sales brochures ready to make some calls for the rest of the day. Making sure the case with the stones was securely stored in the hotels safe deposit. My first call was to a wholesaler in the Luxembourg area, this suburb of Paris is a combination of offices, student accommodation for the nearby university and some exquisite little restaurants. I bought a Carnet of tickets for the Metro, and took this wonderfully efficient railway system to Luxembourg. From the Opera you have to change trains at Les Halles which was to be my second stop for the day, Les Halles is the central market place of Paris, although there are rumours that it will be demolished to make way for a new shopping centre later in the decade.

Exiting the station at Luxembourg and walking South along Boulevard Du Luxembourg the sun was slightly warm and inviting. I was early for my 11am appointment so decided to stop at a café and have a "Pression" Espresso coffee, sitting outside even though it was cool is one of those things you do in Paris to enjoy the world passing you by. The smell of the city is something heady and intoxicating, the well dressed Parisians walking past and the noise of the chaotic traffic all adds to the experience. As I was breathing in this mixture a voice behind me broke my reverie, "You must be at Gare De L'est at 6:30 tonight, go to the baggage lockers and put the case in locker 129" I turned and saw a man in a black leather coat with his back turned to me walking off in to the crowd. He was quickly swallowed by the passing melee of people.

A strange way to pass on instructions I mused, then I realised that I must be being followed all the time. It told me to be on my guard and not allow myself to think I could relax for one moment.

The rest of the day was routine, the wholesalers were reasonably receptive to my sales pitch and I ended up the day with 2 nice orders for bulk shipments. I got back to the hotel at 4:30, laid on the bed for half an hour then changed and got the case from the safe at reception and went back to the Metro station for the journey to Gare De L'est.

Strangely the two railway stations Gare Du Nord and L'est are not that far apart and are on the same line to Porte De Clignanacourt you have to change trains at Reaumur Sebastopol, and whilst doing so I thought I caught a glimpse of the man in the leather coat about 50 metres behind me. Not surprising I was being followed, but by the same person seemed a bit obvious. Anyway, it took about 40 minutes to get there, so I had plenty of time, it was about 5:55 as I walked into the station. Gare De L'est was built in 1849 and is one of the largest and oldest railway stations in Paris. It started out life as the main line to Strasbourg, since then it has seen the Orient Express, and regular services to Alsace and the Champagne region. As you would imagine it has plenty of atmosphere and you can sense the history in the place. How many tears of sadness and happiness have been shed at this place I pondered? I walked out of the glass roofed departure hall to the front of the station to the Boulevard De Strasbourg to look at the fabulous architecture and ornate exterior that is so evocative of those early days of steam rail travel. I checked my watch it was 6:25, so I walked back to the departure hall and went into the locker area, locker 129 was open and had a key in it, and I put the case in and locked it, taking the key with me expecting to have to drop it off somewhere or even mail it. As I went back to the departure hall I heard the public address calling my name to the enquiry desk, I went over to the desk and announced who I was. "Messieur Ellis you have a key to deposit here I understand?" The clerk queried. "Well yes I suppose I do, but do I get a receipt or something?" The clerk handed me a manila envelope telling me a receipt was inside. I handed the key over and walked away somewhat mystified. I decided to just go back to the

Hotel and see what happened next, but could not help looking back to the enquiry desk which now had nobody at the desk and the Closed/Ferme/\Geschlossen sign on it.

As I sat on the Metro I couldn't help but open the envelope, there was yet another smaller envelope inside with a note loose beside it. I read the note "Mr Ellis, you have done well, here is a small token of appreciation for you to help you on your way" There was no signature and it was typed. I opened the smaller envelope, it contained US dollar bills. Back at the hotel I counted $10,000 in 100 bills. I rang Ton using the scrambler and told him exactly what had happened. He told me to return on the first train tomorrow and he would meet me at Centraal Station in Amsterdam, I told him I would ring him back as soon as I knew what train I was booked on. I asked him what I should do with the money and he laughed "Do what you like! It's your money"

I rang the concierge and asked him to book me the first available train in the morning (Friday), five minutes later he rang back saying the earliest was the Trans Europ Express "Etoile Du Nord" at 07:20 from Gare Du Nord and it would arrive in Amsterdam at 13:50. I rang Ton back and he said he would be there.

In the morning I just got up, checked out, and took a taxi to Gare Du Nord. The Trans Europ Express is a First Class only express train service that operates between a number of European cities with minimal stops, this particular train's route was to be Paris Nord-Bruxelles Midi-Brussel Noord-Antwerpen Oost-Roosendaal-Rotterdam-Den Haag HS-Amsterdam. As the train pulled out of the station I ordered breakfast from the waiter and looked forward to my first coffee of the day.

The croissant was exquisite with breakfast but what could one expect on a first class train from Paris? I sat back and watched the suburbs of this great city roll past my window and all I could think was that I would be in the arms of my wonderful Diny tonight. I fell into a deep sleep and must have slept for several hours because we were well into the flat border country of Belgium when I woke up, Belgium is not a spectacular country as far as scenery goes, and it slipped away and merged into the landscape of South Holland, I was at least back in a country where I was not a stranger. The rest of the trip was uneventful and I was relieved to see the outer suburbs of Amsterdam and as the train pulled into Centraal Station I was happy to be home.

Ton met me at the station exit and we took the tram back to his place, we entered his front door and there was Diny with a big smile and open arms. "Oh God it's so good to see you!" I exclaimed. Ton had arranged for Diny to come over earlier in the day and I thanked him for that.

"Robert, Go back to Aalsmeer with Diny have a good rest and we will talk tomorrow afternoon. I will come over and see you" He instructed. We took the bus back to Aalsmeer and Diny insisted that I spend the night at her house, Anje and Hans seemed as relieved as Diny to see me and greeted me with a glass of Lafite as we sat down and relaxed. "It's nice to be home!" I stated and they smiled. Anje broke the silence "Robert we know you are working very hard and want the best for Diny but don't forget to enjoy what you have right now" She cautioned.

We had a wonderful evening together and Hans asked me to enjoy a glass of Cognac with him after dinner and when we were alone, and the two women were going to bed.

"Robert, what exactly is going on? I want to know just why the accident happened, because I don't think it was an accident. Also, why the military presence was so heavy at the hospital? That was not just a precautionary guard, it was serious protection!"

"Hans, you are right." I decided to tell him the truth although Ton would disapprove. "I am in the middle of a serious international crisis that will unfold very soon. It may change the way we live in the future. I'm not being overdramatic about what is at stake. I can't tell you the details, but it involves my father and the secret work he is doing"

Hans shook his head and took a big gulp of cognac and refilled my glass. "Robert, I understand you can't tell me anymore, but I just want you to know as someone who served in the army corps earlier in my life, I am completely behind whatever it is you are able to do to protect our way of life and I admire your commitment!"

"I thought you were going to tear me to bits about it Hans!" I declared. "I mean I'm not sure what the end result will be, but I just have to do whatever I need to, in order to protect what so many Dutch and British people fought and lost lives for in the war if nothing else. But also to be able to look after Diny and you and Anje and all the other friends we have, it's so precious"

He nodded, and suggested we change the subject after agreeing not to let Anje and Diny know what we had discussed. We talked about the weather and the fact that spring was just around the corner and the trip to Portugal after Easter would be a great chance for Diny and I to spend some time together. We finished our cognacs and we went upstairs. I wanted to sleep so much, but the sight of Diny lying in bed waiting for me was too much to resist. She kissed me and tore my clothes off me and proceeded to make love like a woman possessed. We then fell in to a deep sleep and I didn't wake until she opened the curtains and it was 8:30.

"I have to talk to Ton today, he will ring and tell me when he's coming over" I told her over breakfast. "But it's Saturday!" She pleaded. "I was hoping to have you all to myself today" She chided. "Well, I tell you what, I'll ring Ton and see if we can't go to his place, then we can go into Amsterdam and do some shopping this morning" I was thinking of the money in the envelope and how it would be handy to buy some things for our holiday.

I went into the living room and rang Ton using the scrambler, to see if we could change the meeting and he was happy about that, we were to go to his place at 3pm and then stay and have dinner, he was happy to see Diny again he said with a mischievous tone to his voice. I think he had taken a bit of a fancy to her.

We took the bus and walked up the Damrak from Centraal Station, we sat and had a coffee at one the hundreds of little street cafes that have a glass fronted terrace on the street and soaked up the suns ray's, although it was still windy and cold, the glass enclosure protected us and it was almost as though spring was upon us. I sat there thinking that so much had happened in 4 months since that November ferry trip from England, it was now March and my life had been turned upside down.

We went to C&A to shop, I wanted to buy Diny some summer clothes and some swimwear, it would be warm in Portugal and we were going in late April after Easter, Easter was to fall on 22nd April this year, she picked out a lovely skirt and a couple of tops to go with it. I bought a pair of jeans and a couple of casual shirts. We also bought a bikini for her and I teased that Ton would want her to put it on and she blushed.

We got to Ton's place 10 minutes early and he greeted us with the usual cheery smile, he hugged Diny as if she had been away for months, but I didn't mind that fact that he had a special place in his heart for her. We showed off our purchases and true enough, Ton insisted on Diny trying on the bikini, much to my surprise she did! She looked fabulous in it and we both applauded at the impromptu fashion show.

Ton asked Diny if she would mind if we talked a bit of business first before we had a drink, and told her to stay and listen as it was important for her to hear what he had to say. "You both need to know that this situation has become critical, Diny you know by now that Robert and I have become involved in something that relates to Robert's father and the work he does, you now need to know more because your life and your family's may depend on it." Diny's face went white when he said that.

"You are both targets for assassination and Anje and Hans may also be, it is no longer a wild theory or speculation that certain forces are at play that are trying to overthrow European governments, and those that are involved will also be targets once the job has been done, we need to try and stop these plots to kill heads of state and we have people on the ground all over Europe trying to identify just exactly which hit men have been hired to do the job and take them out before they complete their assigned tasks. Once we know they have been stopped, you and others will be assigned new identities and given safe haven so you will be safe from the obvious fallout of the failed plots." Ton looked sombre as he continued. "It is vital that we identify who is behind this whole thing. Robert, you have not been told this yet and it is absolutely top secret for both of you, but we think that Vladimir Semichastniy head of the KGB and Roger Hollis head of MI5 are both behind this plot, for this reason I can no longer trust our usual line of contact with MI6 and Sir Dick White of MI6 has authorised me to only communicate with him or Duncan Sandys via a special line." He told us that Roger Hollis had been long suspected of being a mole for the Russians and they were now convinced, because of information from John McCone of the CIA.

"Robert, Diny, this is extremely high level stuff and I need you both to know there is a very high risk involved not just for you and those close to you but for the entire European community and the rest of the world." He pleaded. "What unfolds in the coming few weeks will undoubtedly affect the future of the western world and the balance of power. The strange thing is that if we manage to foil this plot no-one may ever know about it, as it will be kept secret and never made public."

"So, Ton why are you now allowing Diny to know about this and I was strictly forbidden before to even mention it?" I was angry at suddenly being confronted with this and had been surprised that Ton would even discuss it like this. "Robert it is for Diny's safety that she needs to know, it would be wrong to keep her in the dark. Diny, what are you thinking right now?" he asked. "I'm frightened in one way and angry in another, frightened that such terrible things are happening, but also angry that Russia wants to make such aggressive changes to our world and in such a violent way" She was shaking as she spoke.

Ton explained further, "The Soviet States have been in turmoil for centuries as history shows, mainly because of the oppression of the people and the absolute power of a handful of Czars and dictators, the current incumbents in government know they have a short time before there is some form of uprising or splitting of the various states that embody the union, the Ukraine and the Latvians want to run their own backyard to name but two and there are many other undercurrents of distrust of Moscow and what it represents, by creating a major upheaval in Europe and taking back Berlin and

East Germany and probably Poland and other countries that neighbour their current borders, they are not only creating a diversion for these troubled influences but they are seen to be taking action that will make them absolute in their power. Once they have achieved what will be a takeover of Europe as we know it, nobody will want to pick a fight with them and the people there will continue to live in fear and be oppressed."

It seemed a bleak outlook that Ton painted and the thought of a Europe under Russian power sent chills down my spine. "Ton do you think by stopping this plot, we will actually stop the Russians, or is it just delaying the inevitable?" I asked.

"What we think may evolve after the failure of their plot is that the Russian states will see the failure of the government and the Soviet Union as we know it will implode, states will want their sovereignty and each country will go its own way. Who knows even Germany may become united once more?" Ton explained.

We discussed various security measures that we should take from here on and Ton gave Diny a phone encoder to use. She agreed we would tell her parents tomorrow evening and swear them to secrecy, I was relieved not to be living a lie from here on and that I no longer needed to keep secrets. "Robert and Diny, you also need to know that if we all come out of this alive, you will have great wealth and new identities should ensure your security. But you will never be able to discuss this with anyone so we will set up a dummy company with a Swiss bank account, so that the money will appear to come from legitimate investments" I could see that whilst I had been away Ton had been busy putting this all together.

We sat and had a drink, and Ton had already got a stew in the slow cooker, which we ate whilst still discussing the incredible possibilities of what might come about in the ensuing weeks. Diny and I made our way to the bus in virtual silence, I think we were both drained by the whole thing and when we got back I said goodnight to her, Anje and Hans, and made my way back to Hadleystraat to prepare for the explanation to them in the morning. What a way to spend Sunday! I thought as I tried to sleep, telling the people you love that their entire future and that of Europe was on the line.

Chapter 18 – It's not what you think!

I walked towards Diny's house with a feeling of despair, and for once I was not looking forward to seeing the family that I normally got excited about being with. We sat and had a coffee Anje and Hans had no idea what we were about to tell them although Hans may have had an inkling after our chat a few nights previous.

"Hans, Anje, we have something serious to tell you" I looked sheepishly at Anje. "Diny is pregnant?' She asked almost with glee. "No, it's not personal in that way, I wish it were as straightforward" Diny started to explain, "There is a plot developing and Robert has become involved due to his father's work, it involves a plan by the Russians to overthrow several European governments, he accidentally became tied up with the people who are planning the financing of the hit men who are to carry out the plan." Anje looked dumbfounded, Hans seemed almost relieved it had come out in the open.

I continued, "We are not certain of the timeline yet but it is due to happen within coming weeks, and if they succeed it will bring about a cataclysmic change of power in the western world. It is being financed with illegal diamonds and there are many senior officials in a number of countries involved. That's really all I can tell you right now."

We all agreed it was a depressing situation. Just a few minutes later there was a knock at the door, it was Ton. "I thought you all might want some moral support? I guess you all know now what is going on?" They nodded. Ton came and sat with us and Hans poured him a Cognac. "Ton what I don't understand is why senior government officials from our side are supporting such a thing?" "Robert, they are people who have been around government corridors for their entire career and they have become accustomed to a high lifestyle and lots of power in their hands, they have been promised even greater rewards and more power and are intoxicated by the possibility."

"Ton what will Russia do if we succeed and they get angry about the failure of their plot?" I queried. "We don't know, but we do know they are already angry at the US for building U2 bases in Turkey, so they can spy on the Russian bases within their own territory, so I wouldn't put it past Khrushchev to up the anti and try something else". We sat in silence for a moment and

Hans poured us all another Cognac remarking that we'd better drink it up before the Russians took it over and that made us all laugh and for some insane reason it felt like we had a party going. Ton stayed another hour and we talked about everything except what was bothering all our minds.

The next day, work seemed an interminable drudge, I could think of nothing else but the search for the hired assassins that were being hunted by various undercover agencies and the faint hope that they might be discovered before their deadly tasks were completed. As I rode home on my bike, I breathed in the cool fresh spring air, it had a delicious damp feel to it that European spring evenings possess, that promises warmer and cosier days ahead. When I arrived at Hadleystraat there was a British military Land Rover parked out front, not the kind of vehicle that was normal in this street.

Ralph was sipping a cup of coffee with Miep. "Robert, Ralph has been telling me he works with your father and was driving past and dropped in to see you" She was quite excited that someone from England was visiting. I was not so glad to see him but put on a brave face. "Yes Miep, Ralph is a family friend" He asked if we could go and get something to eat and have a talk, which was a good way to get me out of the house without arousing suspicions that all may not be as it seemed.

We went to "De Uil" on the Uiterweg and ordered a glass of wine each and something to eat. Ralph took over the conversation "Robert, all is not what you think it is." "Ralph I thought we had stopped talking in riddles" I was getting tired of his style of talking down to me all the time. He continued, ignoring my insolence. "The plot to kill these heads of state is not a simple hitman project, but one that involves a suicide attack that may result in many more casualties than just the intended target. We discovered this only a few hours ago when we intercepted one of the perpetrators hired for the job in Spain. He decided to tell us all he knew with a little help from our friend Sodium Thiopental"

I tried to picture the interrogation that resulted in this discovery and it was not something I considered an attractive way to get information from any human being, however Ralph continued and interrupted my thoughts. "We now believe that they have set up cells of people to carry out these acts, mostly recruited from Algeria, the mercenaries that are fighting there are always keen to earn an extra pound or two, and at the same time spread chaos to the rest of world. Their world has been for them, nothing but chaotic for years" He explained the reason he was telling me all this was so I could possibly pick up snippets of information that may put the puzzle together, and help identify where the other cells might be. "So Robert, it's time for you to play out a little set piece we have designed just for you" He spoke as if telling a child there was a cupcake in the secret cupboard downstairs, God I hate this man! I thought.

Ralph went on to outline just what they wanted me to do and not to try and improvise any changes of my own to the plan. He then dropped me back at Hadleystraat and drove off into the night. As I climbed the stairs to my room I felt as though a huge weight had been placed on my shoulders and the more I thought about it the more I realised that is just what it was.

Chapter 19 – God I wish I could go back!

There's an old saying, "don't regret your past, just look toward your future." When you are in your late teens it's not an easy adage to live by because you don't have the skills to understand what that really means. I woke the next morning and felt like a truck had rolled over me during the night, I had not slept well, worrying about Ralph's plan.

I showered and went downstairs and ate breakfast whilst Miep scurried about getting laundry ready. I got on my bike and headed to work, when I got to the office, I asked Gerritt if Jaap was coming in today and he said he was. At around 8:50 Jaap came into the office, I told him I needed to talk to him and we both made excuses that we had some sales plans to talk about and went down into Aalsmeer to a café opposite the Gemeentehuis (town hall), we ordered two coffees and sat at a table at the back. "What is the matter Robert you look worried?" "Jaap, I think I was followed in Paris" He laughed "of course you were, one of our agents had you in his sight all the time!" He was still laughing. "No Jaap, the British were also on my tail, and I think they know what I was doing. When I went to drop the stones I saw not only your man on the train, but an agent I know that works for MI6" He laughed again, "Well you don't need to worry about that, we have very good connections there too!' He was almost gloating at my apparent concern for a situation he knew they had under control.

"Jaap, it's getting very difficult for me to understand who is who in this mess, I need to understand what is precisely going to happen" I stammered. "OK Robert, I will tell you this, we are very impressed that you have carried out your tasks for us in a very efficient way and the little extra we arranged for you to have was by way of a thank you for that. There are going to be dramatic changes in Europe shortly, within a week there will be such turmoil that will engulf everyone and we will ensure that you are looked after as well as Diny and her family, once the changes have taken place you will all be rewarded with privileges you could not dream about. We will arrange for that to happen. But first you must help us further, and you must keep this strictly to yourself. You will be asked to go to Berlin on your own on Thursday to sign a new client, once there you will be given a package, which you will bring back here. Once I have this package your job will be done."

"More diamonds in the package?" I asked. "No, it will be a suitcase and it will be locked, under no circumstances should you let anyone try to open it" It was an order not a request. "I understand Jaap, but what do I do if customs ask to open it?"

"They won't, we have people there who will ensure you are not bothered." He was quite firm about this. "Ok Jaap, I understand, where do I pick up the package?" "It will be delivered to you at the hotel, and once you have it you will go to the airport and leave for Amsterdam, you will keep it with you at all times, until I meet you and take charge of it."

I was confused and angry that he clearly did not or couldn't share with me, the actual nature of what was in the mystery package. I was also concerned that I would be caught by some official who was not in their pay, who would demand I open the package to which I had no keys, and the whole thing would fall about my ears at that point. I guess I'm one of those people who always see the possibility of what can go wrong rather than what can go right.

The only thing I could do was to agree to what they asked of me and continue to put a brave face on what seemed to me to be a hopeless scenario. I went home to Hadleystraat that evening, feeling very concerned not only about my own fate and those around me but of the world in general. My mood was broken by Miep's welcoming smile and an announcement that "Erwtensoup" was for dinner! The world was not that bad after all.

The next day, I went to work and during the day I got the instructions to go to collect my tickets for Berlin and that a wholesaler needed to negotiate a new deal and discounts for pre-packs for the coming autumn season. I knew this was just an excuse but it was also genuine in a way because I did actually have to do the negotiating as well as pick up the package.

Wednesday ran its routine run and in a way I was actually looking forward to the trip to Berlin, I would be on my own and could enjoy the trip. Although I had only been in the job for 5 months, I felt I was a fairly creditable sales person for the company, and was looking forward to travelling on my own.

I got back to Hadleystraat and packed before going down to dinner, Diny came round and joined us. It was a happy evening and Diny went home after watching a movie "Casablanca" with Humphrey Bogart & Ingrid Bergman. What a story of spies and subterfuge I thought, nothing changes! I was tired and I slept well.

I woke at 5:30am and washed and dressed, called a taxi to take me to Schiphol, and was out of the door by 6:15. My flight was for 9am, but I wanted to have breakfast at the airport. It was only when I got in the taxi and looked at my ticket that I realised I had been booked First Class, so resolved to enjoy the moment. I checked in at the VIP check in and was shown to the First Class lounge where a full cooked breakfast buffet was available, so I tucked in to waffles and raisin toast with juice and coffee. Sat back and picked up a copy of the English Daily Telegraph, yesterdays copy, to read about the turmoil still going on in the southern states of USA. Black versus white, East versus West, I pondered as to why it is that those in authority always seem to want to discriminate against other cultures and treat them as enemies, when all the real people want is to live together in relative peace and get on with their lives.

My flight was called and I walked towards the trusty KLM Electra, sat back in my leather seat and enjoyed the prospect of an hour or so completely removed from terrestrial problems. I think why I enjoy flying is because the outside world is temporarily removed from the picture and you can sit back, have a drink and enjoy a kind of suspended animation for a while.

The flight was routine and I took a taxi from Tegel to the Boulevarde Hotel and after unpacking my case, took another taxi to the wholesaler's office and locked up a very nice deal for a 2 year contract to supply them with more pre-packs. This was to be a very short trip as my return was booked for the following morning Friday, so as I went back to the hotel I wondered when the package would be delivered or where I might have to pick it up. My question was answered as soon as I got back to the hotel, the concierge handed me a parcel wrapped in brown paper. It was quite heavy. I took it up to my room and put it on the bed, looking at it and wondering what on earth could be in it.

I had an early dinner and had an equally early night, getting to sleep by 9pm. The following morning had a leisurely breakfast and left the hotel around 9am for my 11:00am flight back to Amsterdam. Once checked in at the airport, I went to the first Class lounge, as I showed my boarding pass at the reception desk I looked across the lounge to see Ralph sitting there with his usual self satisfied smile. I approached him, "Do take a seat dear boy" his patronising attitude instantly grating with me. "Ralph, what are you doing here?" "Well, I'll be able to tell you pretty soon my friend, the boys are just checking your parcel right now in the baggage holding area" He gloated. "Ralph, if they suspect the package has been tampered with I'm dead" He gave me a reproachful look "Robert, the package will be put together just as it was before, don't worry. We are trying to check it quickly so as not to delay your flight, but if necessary we can make some excuse about a technical delay"

I must have looked confused because he went on "It's possible this parcel is the key to what they are going to do and how they are going carry out the attacks" He explained. Just then a man in a grey overall came into the lounge and beckoned to Ralph. He went over and spoke to the man and returned to his seat. "The parcel is just as you checked it in and they will not know we have touched it, the seals on the box inside have been set exactly as they were" He got up as if he was going to leave. "Aren't you going to tell me what's in it?" I asked. "No I am not, it's not important for you to know, it's more important for you to deliver it and not know" His answer actually made sense, if I didn't know I couldn't be suspected of tampering with it.

Ralph disappeared and I heard the flight being called, along with all the other passengers we made our way out onto the tarmac and climbed the stairs to the aircraft. The flight back to Schiphol was routine and I enjoyed a glass of Champagne even though it was barely lunchtime. All the way wondering what could be in the parcel.

As I came out of the baggage claim area at Schiphol , Jaap met me and I handed him the parcel. He put it in the boot of the car and I got in the front passenger seat. "You have done very well" He smiled at me. "What happens now Jaap?" I queried. "The contents of this package will change the course of history, that's all you need to know right now. I will take you home and tomorrow you will meet me at work as normal." I concluded that it was better not to ask any more questions. I got back to Hadleystraat about 2pm that Friday and Miep was surprised to see me home so early. I went up to my room after a cup of coffee with her, unpacked and lay on the bed pondering what I might have done to further the ugly intents of these people. But, I had promised Ralph I would stick to our plan and I would carry that commitment through.

I must have fallen asleep, because the next thing I remember was Diny shaking me and asking me to wake up. It was 5:30 and dark outside. "You didn't ring to tell me you were home!" She complained. "I'm sorry my love I was so tired I must have just crashed to sleep" "That's OK" she looked at me as a mother would scold an unruly child. "Anje has some dinner for us, come over and tell us all about your trip. Did you get a contract?" "Yes, a nice one for 2 years, so that will give us a deposit on a house one day maybe" I tried to sound confident, but I wasn't feeling that way.

We walked over to Opheliastraat in relative silence, I suddenly turned to Diny and said "God, I wish we could go back a few months and change things!" She was surprised by my outburst. "You mean change us, what we have done, are you saying you don't love me anymore?" She was close to tears. "No, no of course not, it's not about us it's about what is going on in the world, I fear for us and our children to come, living in a world with a nuclear time bomb ticking away in the background all the time." For once I was voicing my fears and it seemed to have a calming effect on me. Diny put her arm around me and we walked on, I felt better now I had said something. "Well, at least you think we might have children one day" She smiled, making a positive out of a negative. "It's fun practising anyway my love" She had that cheeky grin on her face. I cupped her face in my hands and gave her a kiss.

When we got to her house Anje and Hans were in their usual happy mood and we had a drink of wine and sat and I told them about the contract. They were pleased I could tell, that my focus was still on getting my job done and when I told them I was saving for a deposit on a house they were impressed. We had dinner and after sat and had a cognac together, Hans asked what was happening with the "other matter". I told them that I was going to see Ton tomorrow (Sat) to find out what was going on. "Diny, if you like we can go together, Ton would be pleased to see you" She nodded and we agreed we would go into the city mid morning and have lunch with Ton. As I walked home I felt better knowing I had such a nice family that I almost considered myself part of now.

Chapter 20 – This is Radio Veronica!

As I went over to Diny's to pick her up and catch the bus into Amsterdam, I wondered what Ton would have to say If anything, about my trip to Berlin. On the way as we sat in the back of the bus, I explained carefully to Diny what had transpired on the trip, she was as mystified as I was what could have been in the parcel. We went to Centraal Station and took tram no 24 to Beethovenstraat and arrived at Ton's door around 11:30. He greeted us with his cheery welcome and already had coffee brewed. He gave Diny a big hug and we sat and enjoyed the coffee and some left over speculaas biscuits from Christmas.

"You two no doubt want to know what the latest news is, so I will waste no time in saying the parcel you brought from Berlin does indeed play a major role in the plan to change Europe. The parcel contained Ricin, which if you don't know is derived from the castor oil bean, and is extremely toxic, it can be inhaled, injected or ingested, and there is no known antidote. Because it is easy and cheap to make, they have decided to use this as the method of taking out the heads of state they have targeted. The problem is whichever way they disperse it will result in many ordinary people dying as collateral damage at the same time, so it is likelihood they will use suicide agents to carry out the attacks, it's also possible that they will not know that they will also die in the process. Ricin causes a horrible death by shock and by attacking the internal organs causing diarrhoea and a very slow and painful end. The contents of the package when examined at Templehof contained 12 tubes of Ricin so we think that by now each tube has been distributed throughout the European cities involved. We do not know the timetable yet or how these assassins will receive instructions to commence the attacks, but we do know it may only be a few days before it all happens"

We sat grimfaced as Ton painted this terrifying scenario, and there was silence for a few moments "Ton, what do we do next to try and stop them?" I asked. "Keep our eyes and ears open, and report back anything that might be a clue as to how they are going to give the signal to action the plan." Ton looked very worried as he told us this. "To be honest, we don't know how they will do it, but there are agents in every city waiting to intercept these people as soon as we know a timeline." I suddenly felt as though the whole thing was out of control and the Russians would surely succeed in their operation. No more was spoken about the operation as we solemnly ate some sandwiches Ton had made. We left his place about 2:30 both of us agreeing it was not for anyone else's ears to know what we had learned. We took the tram back to Centraal station and waited for a bus back to Aalsmeer.

As were waiting, a black Mercedes stopped and Diny and I were pulled into the back by Jaap. The driver in the front put his foot down and we sped off. He looked angry, "Robert, we know now that you have not been keeping your end of the bargain. That package was tampered with at Berlin, one of the seals was not put back correctly, we know it was not you that directly opened it, but we think it might have been British agents and we now know you have been contacted by them. Just what did you tell them?" He demanded, as he spoke he produced a gun and put it to Diny's head. "If you do not come clean, she dies right now!" He was not bluffing.

"Jaap, you know my father works on some of these projects you have been interested in, and I don't know why you haven't confronted me before about it, but I have been coerced into telling them about my trips on your behalf, however I have not told them about the trip to Berlin, they were just there, so I guess they followed me. I had no idea they were going to examine the package and I still don't know what was in it" I was praying he would take the answer as genuine.

"Yes we do know about your father he was one of the few that couldn't be bribed in his department. We wanted to keep our options open with you in case we need to blackmail someone in the MOD, but now we don't need to, and the contents of the package are now split up and are in position all over Europe. We are going to keep you two in safe keeping until this is all over just in case you are lying, we would like to think you were just pressured into this and that you really were trying to help but just in case you will stay with me and then we will decide what to do with you when it's all over. You have been of great assistance and I personally believe your story, but there are others who do not." Good, I thought, he's taken the bait!

We drove on out of Amsterdam and headed South along the road to Rotterdam. We rode in silence except for the radio that was tuned to Radio Veronica a Dutch pirate radio station that had started up a few years before.

I was not prepared to inflame Jaap anymore, so said nothing. Diny cuddled in to my right shoulder, I could tell she was terrified. We arrived at the outskirts of Rotterdam and drove on, turned off the main highway and headed to the docks area. The car rolled down a road and onto a wharf, coming to a stop beside a small tug, the kind used to pilot large ships in and out of the port. We were hustled on board and taken below, pushed into a small locker room and the door clanged shut and a lock was pulled over the door with a loud clunk.

"Oh my god! Diny gasped, what is happening?" I tried to calm her by holding her but she was shaking in terror. It was cold in the locker and dark. I tried to locate a light switch but there was none. A few minutes later the sound of the diesel engine powering up and the tug started to move out from the wharf. Around 10 minutes later I could feel we were heading out to sea because the tug started to pitch in the swell.

After about 10 more minutes we heard the door lock moving and the door was opened by Jaap, "Come up now with me to the bridge we are out in the North Sea" He still had his gun in his waist band, so I decided not to try anything. We got to the bridge and there was Kurt standing behind the helmsman giving him bearings as to where to go. "Hello my friends, we are going to show you now the demise of European rule as we know it and the resurrection of socialism in its truest form, the people will once again own the wealth." I concluded from this that Kurt was completely mad and had totally lost his marbles.

Jaap interjected "What Kurt is trying to explain is that tonight, various European countries will fall into our control and The Soviet Union will once again be a great power. We are going to give the signal that will instigate the operation" "From this ship?" I asked. "No, we are on our way to a ship that has far greater capacity to get our message out" After about half an hour the tug crested a few waves and the navigation lights of another ship could be seen, a few minutes later the outline of the ship was visible, then we were alongside. I could just make out the name of the ship as we came alongside "Borkum Riff".

Jaap and Kurt ushered us out onto the deck of the tug and a rope ladder was thrown over the side of the Borkum Riff, the tug moved up and down in the swell and it was a struggle to lay hands on the ladder and haul ourselves up to the deck of the much larger vessel. "Robert, Diny, welcome aboard, this is Radio Veronica!" Kurt exclaimed. It suddenly dawned on me this was how they were going to transmit the signal to all the agents they had in place. "Jaap, this station surely can't be heard all over Europe? It doesn't have the broadcasting power" Jaap smiled "Just wait and see my friend it soon will have"

A crane on the side of the ship lowered a hook to the tug and one of the crew attached a large box to it, the crane pulled up the box and then lowered it onto the deck. Jaap and Kurt went over and started to lift the lid of the box removing various smaller boxes and taking them down below. We just stood and stared, there was nothing we could do right now. After Jaap and Kurt had unpacked all the contents of the box they ushered us up to the bridge, where a number of the crew were waiting. Jaap started to address everyone "The upgrading of the transmitter is now in progress, shortly we will have a temporary output of 50,000 watts on the 1639 KHz band which will get our signal into just about every European country."

Jaap turned to us and said "Time for you two to take a break" He pushed us out of the bridge and onto the deck walkway towards the midships, we entered a cabin where there were 2 bunks and a table which had some food on it. He said nothing, left, and locked the door. We ate the food it was just some cheese and biscuits but we were hungry. "Robert what can we do to stop this crazy plan?' Diny was fired up now and no longer thought about her fears. "We need to take out the transmitter somehow, and make sure the message does not get out." I said thinking it was easy to say but not so easy to achieve. "I've done a bit of electronics at school and messed about a bit with radio transmitters" Diny volunteered. "So what do we need to sabotage?" I asked. "The antenna would be the obvious thing to disable, but that would be up the mast and probably quite dangerous to mess around with. Wherever they have put the new transmitter is where we need to be so we can disable that equipment."

"So, we need to first of all find a way out of here and then locate the equipment, it's easier now its night time so we need to move quickly." She was quite focused on the job at hand and very confident. "Look Robert, the air duct in the ceiling, one of us could climb up there and the other create a diversion whilst the equipment is tampered with! I'm thinner than you so it makes sense if I go, they would have put the equipment in the area they first took it to, which is the next group of cabins towards the rear of the ship. That must be where the radio room is. I know enough to disable the transmitter without them realising, if you create a commotion about 10 minutes after I leave, that will give me enough time to get back here and they will never know." Diny was quite definite in her sense of purpose and I admired a side of her I had not seen before, she was quite feisty about all this.

"OK as long as you take great care it's really the only hope we have of stopping them. I wish we could get a message to Ton" "The ship may have a radio telephone, if it does I'll try and call him" She said. She climbed up on the bunk bed and started to open the grill to the air vent, the vent was not easy to prise open and it had some screws on the upper side retaining it. With the noise of the sea and the generator in the background we hit the grill with the chair leg hoping it would not be heard. The grill came away clattering to the floor. Diny climbed up into the air duct it was a tight fit even for her tiny body, she started to wiggle her way along the duct and I pushed the grill back into place once I was sure she had gone. I suddenly realised I had not taken the time to say goodbye or give her a kiss, but she was now the only hope of reversing the inevitable, so my thoughts were only of how she was going to get to the radio room and how she might get in there when nobody was about. So I started to plan what type of diversion I would create, one that would ensure all crew members would come running. There is only one big threat at sea, Fire! So I decided that would be the diversion. I started to put all the blankets and pillows in a heap on the floor, how could I set light to them? I wondered. There was an electric radiator under the bed, so I stuck a sheet over it and turned it on. Once alight I decided the chairs and table would be a good addition, once there was a reasonable fire I would bang on the door and try to kick it out. There was a smoke alarm in the cabin, so would presumably set off some type of alarm somewhere. 8 minutes passed and I could smell the sheet stuck over the radiator getting hot but still no flame. Smoke started to come from under the bed, and suddenly the sheet burst into flame. I put a pillow on it and that started to burn, then the wooden chair started to singe and an acrid smell came from it. The table and the other chairs were next, suddenly the whole cabin was engulfed in fire and the alarm sounded, I started to kick at the door and yell for help, one of the crew was the first to arrive but he did not have a key, so yelled for help. I lay on the floor by the door to get air. I heard Jaap's voice as he ran toward the cabin. He unlocked the door and a wall of flame rushed out of the door.

The whole crew was here now and I heard fire extinguishers being taken off their hooks on the outside wall. I lay in the corner of the room near the door, and prayed that Diny would make it back in time, suddenly the grill came clattering down and she jumped down from the duct onto the floor, landing almost by my side. We both covered our faces with our clothes and rushed out, to be held by some crew members. Jaap came up to us and demanded what was going on. "Why did you set fire to the cabin?!" He roared. "We didn't, the heater must have had a sheet touching it and because it was so cold I turned it up. That must have caused it" I pleaded.

The crew fired the extinguishers into the cabin and quickly got the fire under control. Jaap herded us into a cabin in the next block down, the same block as the radio room, he came in with us and sat on one of the bunks. "I don't know if I believe your story, but there seems no other source of the fire at this stage so I guess I have to believe you in which case you are lucky to be alive. Either way, you will stay here until the operation is complete, we will then decide what to do with you. You are either heroes or trying to subvert this mission and I'm not sure whether to kill you or give you a medal" Jaap was obviously stressed and was not happy that we seemed to be a liability to him. This is exactly the kind of pressure that Ralph wanted me to put on these guys, the plan was taking shape.

After Jaap locked us in the cabin I turned to Diny and we kissed without a word spoken. I breathed in her scent and was happy she was alive. "Did you manage to do anything?" I queried. "Yes, their transmitter now has some broken circuits courtesy of some cut wires to the output stage of the unit, I cut them at the back so they won't be noticed until someone checks, by then it should be too late. But there is no radio telephone so we can't let anyone know where we are.

Chapter 21 – It's Going to Be Rough!

We sat on the edge of the bunks, wondering what the timeline would be for the operation to commence, it was now around 10:30pm so it was anyone's guess when they would try to send the signal. Around 15 minutes later Jaap appeared with some coffee for us, he came in and sat at the table. "I'm sorry if I didn't believe you before but I was worried that the whole operation would be in jeopardy if the ship was on fire, and I really thought you had set fire to it. The crew checked the cabin and confirmed that electric heater had been playing up for a while so it must have been the cause. You realise you are about to be part of history you two?" He asked. "Jaap, just what is going to happen?" Not thinking for one moment he would tell us. "In about half an hour we will start the transmitter and a few minutes after it has reached full power one of the regular DJ's will play "Bring it on home to me" by Sam Cooke from last year's top ten, and at the end he will just say "Bring it on home" that will trigger all our agents to go into action, by morning the job will be done" He grinned as he said that.

"I can't tell you what will happen after that but it's going to be rough for a few weeks while governments are sorted out and peace is restored, the general public will take some time to come to terms with a Europe under Communist rule, but they will have to accept it. Once the initial takeover of Berlin has happened Marshall Law will be declared and a night time curfew imposed whilst the military move into position in each country. Then each local government will be given the responsibility of keeping law and order with the help from the military."

"You two will probably be offered a place to live and enough money to live well, as long as you keep in line, if you do not you may not live long" Jaap was telling us more than we needed to know but it seemed like he needed to tell someone. "Jaap what do you think the USA will do once this has happened?" "They will have no choice but to surrender to us or be wiped out by the technology they have helped to develop" He was obviously referring to the stolen plans for the guidance systems. "I have to go and get ready for the start of the operation" he walked out of the cabin and locked the door as he left.

"Well, now we know, let's just hope your sabotage works my love" I smiled at Diny We heard activity in the radio room behind us, the whirr of the portable generator for the additional power to the transmitter, the sound of people coming from various directions past our cabin. The music coming from the monitor in the radio room was turned up, it was difficult to make out the muffled sounds, but the bass could be heard. The deadline of 11:30 was fast approaching and there was nothing more we could do.

As 11:30 came and went, we both wondered what could be going on in the radio room, suddenly there was loud bang from that direction and a man let out a loud scream of pain. There was a second blast much louder and it shook the ship, several yells of fire by some of the crew, scampering feet were heard passing our cabin, one man screamed to get more fire extinguishers, I recollected seeing 3 being used in our previous fire, so there were none left in this area of the ship. Diny muttered something about the output stage having been overloaded and blowing, but right now the heat from the fire was coming through the wall of the cabin from the radio room behind us, I could smell smoke and an acrid smell of plastic burning. "It's the electric conduit burning, we need to get out of here, and the toxic fumes will kill us" Diny screamed. I tried to kick out the door but it was an inward opening door and there was no way I could get it loose. We lay on the floor with fumes swirling above us coming in via the air duct, I covered both our heads with a blanket. It was getting difficult to breath and the fire was now taking hold behind us, I could hear furniture crackling and more bangs as other electrical equipment blew up. The lights failed plunging everything into darkness. Then emergency lights came on, just enough to see the cabin and the ever increasing cloud of fumes. Suddenly the general alarm sounded a series of short bursts on the ships horn, people outside were screaming to abandon ship. It was obvious in the chaos we had been forgotten about.

The door suddenly burst open, it was Jaap. "Come on you two get out and go to the stern of the ship and wait for me, the transmitter has blown, it must have been damaged on the way out here" At least we weren't being blamed for it yet. We scurried out trying to catch our breath, and made our way down the portside to the stern where several crew were deploying life rafts and one lifeboat. Jaap followed behind us with his gun in his hand. We got to the stern and looked back to see the entire cabin section where we had been alight. Some crew were still trying to douse the flames, but it was a losing battle. "I told them to check the god dam transmitter before we brought it out here, but they said there was no time" Jaap complained.

Diny said to Jaap "Is there a normal ships radio on the bridge?" Jaap nodded. "Well, we could at least try and call for help on that before the ship is totally engulfed by fire" She suggested. Jaap nodded and said it was worth a try. The three of us went forward towards the bridge, but we had to get past the burning midships, the heat was intense and I touched the railing and felt it burn my hand. We ran past the most intense part of the fire and sped towards the staircase to the bridge. As we entered the bridge itself Diny closed the door and we looked back at the stricken ship. "Here is the radio, I think it works off a separate battery so it should be OK for a short time" Jaap said. Diny grabbed the handheld mike and tuned the unit to 500Khz the international distress frequency, she called "Pan Pan Pan this is motor vessel Borkum Riff we have a fire on board and require immediate assistance, over" There was silence, then a voice "Borkum Riff this is Coastguard station Rotterdam port, state your position and bearing please" "Oh god, where are we?" Diny screamed at us both. "Get some charts or something" Jaap and I went to the locker at the rear of the bridge to try and find a chart. Suddenly there was a huge explosion and the entire ship shuddered. "The engine room has blown!" exclaimed Jaap. I opened a locker and found a chart, took it over to the light at the helm, thank god I had done a shore based navigation course when I was younger and keen to do some yachting. I took a protractor and based on the current compass and a rough guess that we were at least 12 miles out off the coast outside the national Dutch limit I took a chance and yelled some coordinates to Diny who relayed them over the radio. Suddenly the radio gave out, the batteries were dead. We had no idea if those co-ordinates had been heard. What do we do now?" Demanded Jaap. "We wait" I said.

Chapter 22 - Thank God for the Royal Navy

About 15 minutes passed and we all tried to gather our composure. Suddenly a high intensity searchlight completely illuminated the entire ship, and a loudspeaker system boomed out "This is Her Majesty's Submarine Dreadnought, please stay where you are, put your hands on your heads and await our boarding party, anyone with firearms should put them on the ground, you will be shot on sight if you have a firearm in your possession" Two groups of marines clambered up each side of the ship with large fire extinguishers in their hands and others were armed. They had the midships fire under control in minutes, and had everyone rounded up very quickly.

A couple of the marines herded Diny and myself off the ship at gunpoint without even speaking a word, we climbed down a ladder onto the deck of the huge submarine and we climbed up to the conning tower and down into the hull of the ship. We were greeted by Commander Sambourne "Welcome aboard my ship Mr Ellis, you have the admiration of some of my crew with your endeavours tonight!" He had a really genuine smile on his face "Well you have this young lady to thank for a lot of it sir" I pointed to Diny and he shook her hand.

"You are the first non naval visitors aboard my ship we will have to give you the tour later, we only started sea trials a few days ago and are not yet commissioned, but this task was allocated to us and we were happy to help" "What task?" I asked. "We have been on station for a number of hours below the surface Robert, you see we had the tug plotted on radar the moment it left port" a familiar voice that I did not expect to hear and Ralph appeared out of nowhere he had that silly smirk on his face. "You have done extremely well Robert congratulations, Kurt had a document on him that gave us the location of all the agents, and are being rounded up as we speak. The threat is now a lot lower thanks to your endeavours" "You mean you knew where we were all along?" I asked. "Of course, but we were not expecting you to make it so easy for us to take the ship, we had a whole brigade of marines on board in case it got tough, but thanks to you not a shot was fired!" We were escorted below and shown to a cabin, some fresh clothes and a shower later, we both felt like human beings again. We were shown to the officers mess and introduced to the senior officers by Commander Sambourne, and given a hearty meal with a ration of navy rum on the side.

As we ate, Commander Sambourne explained that Dreadnought was a totally new ship and the first nuclear powered submarine in the British Navy, she would be commissioned in April and would go into immediate service. He joked that the Russians would love to get their hands on these blueprints if not for anything else but the state of the art sonar devices on board. After our meal we were shown around the ship, it was huge and seemingly roomy for a submarine. He explained it was capable of staying submerged for many months at a time and had nuclear strike capabilities. An amazing war machine that I hoped would never be used in anger.

Ralph told us it was time to go, we said our farewells and we went up through the conning tower, we were greeted by the clatter of a navy Sea King helicopter above us, a large basket was lowered and First Diny, then myself and Ralph were hoisted up to the chopper. As soon as were all on board the Sea King made a fast climb and sped to the coastline. We arrived at the Royal Dutch Navy base at Valkenburg. From there a car took us to the British embassy in The Hague. Ralph explained that although it was late we needed to do an immediate debrief. We were shown into a large conference room just the three of us and coffee and biscuits were brought in. Ralph explained he needed to record everything we had done and wrote it all down on a notepad as we told him everything since being whisked away at Centraal Station.

"What will happen to Jaap and Kurt?" I asked. "They will be locked away for good and kept at a secret location" Ralph said. "And what about the Borkum Riff?" I asked.

"It's repairable, our marines will bring it back to a serviceable state. The owners have been notified there was a fire onboard and that it was just lucky our navy were close by, and that we will get them back on the air as soon as practicable. As I've told you before Robert this operation will never be shown in the history books and we will shortly give you and Diny new identities, you will continue on as if nothing has happened. You will enjoy your holiday in Portugal, the diamonds are yours to keep as well as the money, so you should both be in a comfortable situation financially."

The next day Diny and I were chauffeured back to Aalsmeer and Anje and Hans greeted us with open arms. It took a few days before it dawned on me that the threat was really over and life could go on as normal. The month of March was cold, 1963 was going to be one of the coldest and longest winters in Dutch history, and canals were still frozen over into April. We looked forward to our holiday, Diny studied and I worked through those weeks. Something still bothered me though. I figured the Russians wouldn't just give up their plan to dominate the West, and wondered what they might do next. But a few months went by and nothing seemed to eventuate, so Diny and I went to Monte Gordo and had a great holiday.

The beach hotel there was literally right on the beach and we were woken each morning by the gentle "putt putt" of the local fishing vessels making off for the day to catch local tunny, so we would enjoy charbroiled tuna steaks that night for dinner. We used our rental car one day and went right up into the mountains, stopping at a small village called Cachopo for lunch. It was an idyllic holiday and after 7 days we were so relaxed. We vowed to return one day.

Chapter 23 – It's not over yet!

The summer months passed by, I made a few trips to Belgium for sales. Diny and I visited Ton every weekend and had some great times together, we decided to wait until Autumn before looking for a house to buy. One Saturday in the middle of August we went Ton's house for dinner, he welcomed us in his usual way. But he seemed worried as we sat and had a drink of Jenever.

"What's the matter Ton? You look worried about something" "Well Robert you were right, the Russians have not given up their quest to undermine the West" "Oh God no? Not another plot?" I was alarmed. "Well, not exactly, after the Cuba crisis last year and what we have been through this year, you would think they might give up. But a much bolder plan is unfolding, the Russians are supplying high tech weapons to Vietnam, aircraft and armaments, and we think there will be conflict in Asia before long, we think they are trying to organise the overthrow of President Diem. If there is an Asian war it will be their way of getting a foot in the door via the back entrance so to speak, and it will not be so easy to combat their motives because other cultures are involved and that doesn't mean it will be a simple solution. It will be a long and messy war over which we will have no control but may become involved." We all agreed it was not a pretty scenario. This was to become the Vietnam nightmare!

Endnote

Most of the content in this story is based on fact. The main characters are fictitious but based on people I knew. Some of the military personnel and political characters depicted are factual. There is no intention on the author's part to suggest that Russia actually plotted to overthrow European governments, although there likely was a plan to do so. In the times of the so called "Cold War" anything was possible and probably still is. Ricin is now recognised as a biological warfare weapon and has been used since the 1960's in many recorded terrorist attacks. The "Cold War" may well return in years to come although division in Europe is now less likely with the advent of the EU alliances. But the threat of the use of Nuclear weapons still exists, and in fact quantities of enriched uranium are known to have now fallen into the hands of the likes of Al Qaeda and rogue states such as Iran and North Korea as well as unstable dictatorships. The clock is still stuck at 1 minute to midnight!